LOVER'S MOON

A CANADIAN WEREWOLF NOVEL

MARK LESLIE
JULIE STRAUSS

Stark Publishing

STARK
PUBLISHING

Stark Publishing
Waterloo, ON
www.markleslie.ca

Publisher's Note: This is a work of fiction. Names, characters, places, and incidents are a product of the authors' imagination. Real locales and public and celebrity names are sometimes used for atmospheric purposes. Any resemblance to actual people, living or dead, or to businesses, companies, events, institutions, or locales is either completely coincidental or is used in a completely fictional manner.

Lover's Moon / Mark Leslie & Julie Strauss. -- 1st ed.
Hardcover ISBN: 978-1-989351-70-3
Trade Paperback ISBN: 978-1-989351-69-7
eBook ISBN: 978-1-989351-71-0
Audiobook ISBN: 978-1-989351-72-7

First paper printing May 2022

DEDICATION

For Liz and Joe
Thank you for putting up with us
and with all the imaginary people who live in our heads.

Table of Contents

LOVER'S MOON

Friday, July 28, 2017

Prologue

GAIL

When I first met Michael, it seemed like his skin couldn't hold the pulsing energy inside him. His coiled intensity could hardly be contained.

Now, he's a shell.

That same skin barely holds his broken heart and brittle bones in one place.

Most of the time, I'm taking care of him. I force him to take a shower every day, I help him respond to the most urgent messages from his agent, and we ignore the rest.

He spends hours staring numbly at sitcom reruns and then has no recollection of them afterward.

We have spoken so few words to each other, and almost all of them have been accompanied by tears. During the night, when he thrashes in his sleep, only my touch can soothe him.

When I'm not caring for him, I gaze out the window, watching the oblivious world outside continue on. There is almost certainly a Gail's-ass-shaped groove in the windowsill where I've spent so many hours over the last two weeks.

Every day, I stare at a picture of Lex on his kitchen counter. Her head is thrown back in a laugh—probably at one of Michael's dumb jokes. Her mouth is open wide, and her eyes are crinkled shut. It's not the most flattering image of her; she is—she *was*—a stunning woman, and this image obscures most of her natural beauty. But it is the most accurate photo of her. The most alive. I have been debating moving this photo, unsure if it will make things worse for him. But ultimately, I leave it. That will have to be his choice.

He wakes suddenly, and I move off the windowsill to his side.

He calls her name.

He opens his eyes.

He looks at me. Hopefully. Longingly.

He doesn't want to want me. I see that in his eyes too.

I can almost see his thoughts, like a series of slides projected across his clouded eyes. He must have been dreaming about her—those last seconds, when she let go and fell from his sight.

I stroke his cheek, patchy and unshaven, and run my fingers through his hair. I whisper soft words of reassurance, hum something tuneless. *I'm here*, I say. It is something I have said hundreds, perhaps thousands of times over the last two weeks.

I'm here. It's okay. You're okay.

I'm here.

It's not enough. My God, it's not even close. I'll never be enough.

He fights but eventually falls back to sleep. This is the first time I've understood the phrase *falling asleep*, because Michael is truly falling. I see him fighting it, trying so hard to stay awake. He wants to scream, he wants to fight, he wants to go back in time and change something, but instead he falls into the abyss after Lex. If he could change one moment before the end, it would have turned out differently, and he would not be reliving that moment in these feverish, sweaty dreams he's now having.

If only one thing had gone differently, it might have been me who dropped off that railing.

Or him.

I'm afraid to ask which one he'd prefer.

Once he's slipped back into his dreams, calm for the moment, I resume my position on the windowsill. I'm only wearing his T-shirt and boxer shorts, which I've clipped at the waist so they don't fall down. We haven't left his apartment since it all happened, but I'm going to have to make a move soon, either to get some clothes from my place or to take all of his to the laundromat, since between the two of us we're down to just a couple of clean items left. I pull my knees up to my chin and wrap the shirt over them, down to my ankles, and hug my body into a tight ball. I inhale the familiar scent of his shirt, musky and warm, and then wipe my tears onto the soft fabric.

When I recover, I gaze out on the street again.

I suppose we could stay here indefinitely. I don't think I'd mind it. A tiny part of me likes this suspended moment that we are in together, even though my heart hurts and my face is blotchy from crying, and I've gnawed my once-smooth fingernails down to the skin. We are safe here—as safe as people like us can be. I sleep next to him at night. More than once, I've woken up wrapped in his arms. When that happens I'm caught in a déjà vu so real that it knocks the wind out of me. It always takes me a few minutes to remember that this is now, not then, and he is only holding me out of habit, not any kind of love or desire. Even if it's not love, I would be willing to care for him here forever. Eventually, he'll be well enough to join me on this windowsill. We can watch the oblivious world go by together. We don't need anyone else.

Maybe we never did.

But I can't let that happen.

We have lives that we've utterly disappeared from, but they are still out there. I have to get back to the store, and he has a book deadline. We both have people who love us and are concerned about us.

But I wish we could stay here. I wish we didn't have to face what's next.

He's sleeping deeply now, still and unmoving on the bed, sprawled on his stomach with his arms splayed out to his side. I imagine he's dreaming of holding on to her, that his body reflects his dreams, and he's constantly reaching past me, toward her, trying to pluck her out of the sky and bring her back to earth.

I use this moment to jump into the shower. The hot water courses over my body, and I shiver with the pleasure of it. I'd love to linger here for hours. I'd love to drown in it.

But I don't let myself stay for even a moment longer than necessary. I don't want him to wake up alone.

When he wakes from those terrible dreams, his state of mind could be anything from childlike confusion to rage to despair. I don't want to be responsible for what he might do if I leave him alone for too long. I'm already responsible for too much.

I wrap my hair in a towel and realize I haven't brought any clothes into the bathroom with me, so I open the door quietly to sneak out into the bedroom and grab another one of his shirts. I will have to deal with laundry today, no question.

Though I'm tiptoeing, I glance over at the bed and freeze when I see him sitting up, looking right at me.

I'm so startled by his steady gaze that I can't move.

He looks exactly like the Michael I met six years ago— who stared at me across the Barnes & Noble café.

His eyes widen a bit, and for one horrifying instant I think he was hoping Lex would step out of the bathroom, and now he is disappointed that it's me in his house, in his life.

He's angry that I'm the one left.

But then I realize that, despite everything else going on, Michael is still a horndog of a hetero man, and I'm naked in front of him, and even though he's seen me like this before, it's been a while. I can feel a hot blush climb up my cheeks, and I reach back into the bathroom to grab another towel.

"You're awake," I say, keeping my voice cheerful, as though he just dozed off for a quick catnap instead of a two-week bender.

"I'm awake," he repeats.

I take a deep breath, keep my face neutral, and walk toward the bed, tucking the towel around my body like this is a perfectly normal conversation.

"How are you feeling? Do you want some lunch? Or, no, I guess it's time for dinner? I could get you some..." I drift off.

He's examining me carefully, and for the first time in what feels like years, I can see my Michael again. His dark brown eyes are clear. The urge to reach out and touch his face is so strong that I twist my hands into the towel just to keep them occupied. I'm no longer sure of my place here.

"What day is it?" he asks.

I take a deep breath. "Friday."

"Friday?" he murmurs. I can see him trying to piece it all together. "The same—" he begins, but then he corrects himself. He knows it can't be the same Friday. He knows, but he doesn't want to say it out loud.

"It's the twenty-eighth. Two weeks."

I watch the understanding dawn on him.

"You've," he starts, but then he stops. Swallows. "I've been here the whole time?"

I nod.

"You stayed with me." It's a statement, not a question.

We look at each other, and for a horrifying moment, I think he might ask me to leave.

"You cry in your sleep," he says quietly.

Now I understand why I wake up in his arms. He has also been taking care of me.

I didn't think I had any more tears left inside my body, but they appear again. I look down and wipe them away with my fingertips. "I miss her," I finally say.

"Me too."

We are silent for a moment longer.

I've always been able to read Michael, but he's lost to me now. Maybe Lex will be a ghost between us forever, shimmering in the air, making it impossible for me to see him as clearly as I once did.

Maybe the same is true for Michael. We'll spend the rest of our lives trying to reach each other and never connecting because she'll always be there. Maybe that's what we deserve.

As soon as I have this thought he reaches his hand out and takes mine. We sit that way for a moment, our arms stretched out across the bed, and then he smiles at me.

I laugh at the awkward position and then scoot over to the headboard so I can sit next to him. I have to drop his hand to clasp the towel to my chest, and when I sit back, I wish I had the nerve to touch him again.

That's another change I suppose I'll have to get used to. Before this moment, I'd never been afraid to touch Michael.

Michael is *mine*. He's always been mine. Even Lex knew that. Why can't I touch him?

I pull the towel off my head and let my damp hair down onto my bare shoulders. I see him watching me, but I try to act like this is a very normal day. Two people, broken beyond recognition, who used to know each other inside and out, who now can barely fit two sentences together, sitting on a bed in an apartment they haven't left in two weeks. Oh, and one of them is naked.

It's fine.

"Thank you," he finally says.

"For what?"

He laughs. It's just a short, almost barking noise, but it's the sweetest sound I've ever heard. We are almost MichaelAndGail again, cocooned in our own world, laughing at our stupid private jokes. But then he grows serious.

"For all of it," he says. He nods to the bedroom door, beyond which we can see the neat kitchen. "For taking care of me."

"I would never leave you alone, Michael. You know that."

"Are you okay?" he asks, and I swallow hard past the lump suddenly blocking my throat.

I have no idea which answer to give him. *I miss her too? I've lost a friend? I'm sorry she was the one to die, not me? You are hurting, and so I am hurting?*

"You're back," I finally say. "So, things feel a little bit brighter."

"She loved you, you know."

I nod because I can't answer without crying. I'm twisting the towel so hard I think I might shred it.

"Did you hear her? What she said at the end?"

For a moment I consider lying. I've never once gotten away with lying to him, but I am tempted to do it now if only to avoid this conversation. If I was smart, I'd jump off this bed, get dressed in my own clothes, and leave him here. I could walk away from all of this, and no one, least of all Michael, would fault me for it.

But I've never been able to walk away from him, and he's always spotted my lies. So, I nod again.

I see it deep in your eyes when you look at each other.

She'd known all along.

I finally look up at him and see that his eyes are also brimming with tears.

I curl into him and rest my cheek on his shoulder. His arms come around my body and we are MichaelAndGail again. Part of me can't believe that our bodies still fit together like this.

"I'm sorry," I whisper. I don't say what I'm sorry for. I'm sorry for everything.

"I'm sorry too."

We remain in that position for a long time, my hair slowly drying under his gently stroking hands as we watch the light change outside. I feel our heartbeats sync up, and I don't want to break the spell so I keep still, breathing in his scent, wishing we could hold this moment forever.

Eventually, he stretches, and though I don't want to let him go, I'm glad to see his body come back to life.

I start to pull away from him, but the towel stays hooked under his arm, and I'm naked in front of him.

Suddenly, he doesn't look confused anymore.

I quickly reach for the towel, but Michael's hand stops mine.

"Gail," he says.

My breath catches in my throat. It has been so long since he's said my name like that. I want him to say it again, in exactly that way that he has. Low in the back of his throat, almost like a growl. My bare skin is covered in goose bumps, but I don't move for the towel. I just look at him.

He runs his hand up my arm so slowly I could scream, but I don't let my eyes drop from his.

He reaches my face, strokes his thumb over my lips, and then caresses the back of my neck with his hand.

My breath is coming in fast, shallow gasps.

He hesitates before he leans in to meet me.

Perhaps the confusion reflects on my own face.

For a moment, I can't move.

I'm lost in the familiarity of the mouth that I used to know as well as my own, and I forget to react. But then I snap out of it because my body has come back to life too.

My tongue meets his, and he tastes the same. My need for him overcomes everything, and all at once I forget that I have spent the last two weeks tending to him like an invalid, that we are both grieving, that the world as we know it has changed. I just want him. I want comfort. I want the glorious, ecstatic amnesia his body promises me.

We tumble into the sheets, our limbs entangled, tugging at the towels and his pajamas, feverishly tearing away the thin fabric that separates our skin.

His body is the same, his touch is the same, and I am consumed with my need for him. I wrap my legs around his waist and lock my ankles together behind him, to pull him closer and—yes, I admit it—to keep him there. I'm not exactly proud of this, but I don't want to know if he has second thoughts. I want to keep him here, inside me.

We move in sync, our rhythm familiar but intensified. I am barely aware enough to notice that Lex's shadow is not in the room, and just petty enough to be grateful that it is Michael and me again. The way it used to be.

He moves slowly at first and pulls back slightly to look me in the eye. He grins at me, that sexy sideways smirk that always drove me insane, and I can't help myself; I'm smiling back at him like a fucking idiot. He puts his hands on the bed on either side of my face and arches his back as he thrusts into me, and we explode together, gasping and laughing.

It takes a long time to catch our breath. He's still on top of me and I don't want him to leave.

Finally, he stirs and raises his head to look at me. He pushes the hair out of my face and kisses my forehead. "What did the vampire say when he masturbated in front of a mirror?"

I'm startled by this, but I see the corner of his mouth quirking up in a half grin, and I know he's trying to defuse the situation. I narrow my eyes at him. I've known him long enough to beat him to the punchline.

"Didn't see *that* coming?"

He collapses back into me, and we roar with laughter. My body is spent with the emotions that have roller-coastered through this day, and the confusion is still present. But it feels as if we have finally recovered ourselves. He rolls off me and pulls the bedsheet up over us so we can snuggle into each other. The light slanting into the room has turned from golden to lavender blue, and the sound of the nighttime city bathes his bedroom.

"All this time, since we've been apart," he says, "however long it's been…"

"Five years, eight months, thirteen days," I say promptly. He looks at me with some surprise, and I laugh again. "Or something like that. I haven't really thought about it."

He grins and continues. "All that time, I tried to tell myself our relationship wasn't that great."

"First of all, how dare you?"

"No, *you* were great. I knew that. I just told myself *we* weren't that great. We were just normal amounts of great. But I was fooling myself. I never found anything like this again."

I don't want to break the spell, but I have to. We have to be done with the secrets. "You fell in love again though. Didn't you?"

He nods and smiles, and it's the saddest smile I've ever seen on his face. I want to kiss it away, to keep him from answering, but we have to face it. This time Michael and I will go forward without blinders. I need this answer, and I need the truth.

His nod morphs into a slow shake of the head, his eyes never leaving mine. "Lex wasn't you."

I know this feeling all too well, and my heart aches for the people Michael and I have hurt on our way back to each other.

"Do you ever think about when we met?" I ask him.

"Of course. Do you?"

"All the time. What do you remember?"

"No way," he laughs. "I'm not falling into that trap. I'm going to say I remember that green blouse you were wearing, and then I'm in trouble because it was a blue blouse, and suddenly I'm the asshole."

"It wasn't blue *or* green," I say with mock indignation.

He leans over me and kisses me deeply, and for a moment I forget my name. When he finally pulls away, he dances his finger across the cleft at the base of my throat.

"You had a studded necklace on," he says, and his finger sizzles along my neck and down my chest. "And a lacy shirt, with a collar unbuttoned down to here."

His finger stops below my breasts, almost to my navel, and I know he's wrong; I wouldn't have worn a shirt that low-cut for a business meeting with a stranger. But for once, I don't argue with him. I want him to keep touching me. His hand runs down my flank and he cups my ass.

"You wore black leather pants and a black leather jacket over that crazy shirt. I remember thinking how badly I wanted to peel those clothes off you very slowly."

I am shivering with pleasure at this point and can barely catch my breath. But his hands and his nuzzling have stopped, and he's looking into my eyes again.

"Do you remember what I was wearing?"

"Ummmmm." I look at the ceiling and frown. "It was this sort of loose golf shirt, I think? With light green and yellow stripes? And baggy cargo shorts. You had a tourist map of New York sticking out of your butt pocket. And those shoes. How could I forget those shoes? You don't see too many people in New York wearing knee socks with flip-flops."

I bite my lip hard to keep from smiling, but then I glance at him and laugh anyway. For a second I'm afraid he's going to transform right in front of me out of sheer outrage.

Michael was a lot of things, but a sloppy dresser was never one of them. He'd rather walk through Central Park stark naked than wear loose cargo shorts. When he realizes I'm teasing him, he grins, kisses me, and then jumps out of bed and wraps the towel around his waist.

I pull the sheets up to my neck and sit against the headboard, enjoying the view. I could never have guessed how much pleasure it would give me to see him take the initiative again. I would really like to say I forgot how gorgeous he was, but that would be a lie. I could never have forgotten this. He's pale and thinner, but it's still hard to take my eyes off him.

I see him glance at the photo of Lex, pause, and then pick it up. A small smile crosses his face, and he runs his finger over her dimpled cheek. I'm suddenly so glad I didn't move the picture while he was recovering. Whatever happens to Michael and me, she will be part of our lives forever.

He puts the photo down and takes a deep breath.

"I'm starving," he says. "Are you hungry?"

I can hardly speak, so I nod and watch him start making a mess in the kitchen.

He cooks like he does everything else—banging around too loudly, moving too quickly, not following directions. My stomach growls and my body aches for him again, and I don't know if I want to let him cook for me or leap over the kitchen counter and fuck him against the sink. I feel strangely guilty that I have the option. So I simply watch him, a stupid grin on my face, while he puts handfuls of garlic, onion, and spices in a sizzling pan of oil.

The scent is beyond intoxicating.

Saturday, May 21, 2011

Chapter One

MICHAEL
11:52 a.m.

The scent was beyond intoxicating.

It was so compelling, in fact, that I could almost feel myself getting turned on.

And I hadn't even seen her yet.

The fragrance of basil, oregano, rosemary, and thyme, mixed with garlic, permeated the air. Antonio's Urban Kitchen was the kind of place that would make you hungry regardless of your condition when you walked in.

You could have just come from either a marathon session at an all-you-can-eat buffet or finishing a winning run at Nathan's annual hot dog eating contest on Coney Island and still find yourself suddenly overwhelmed with hunger pangs.

And while the food here was amazingly delicious, the smell of the place was out of this world.

Because I was still in the tail end of my monthly cycle where, after sunset I morphed into my wolfish alter ego, the effect of the delicious smells was that much more intense. Even at the lowest time in the moon phase cycle when my canine-enhanced abilities were at their weakest, they were still at least two to three times more sensitive than a normal human's.

Particularly since I'd realized I hadn't had anything to eat since that stale muffin I'd crammed into my mouth with that morning's coffee. It was normal for me to skip meals and forget to eat when I was in the middle of a writing deadline, which was exactly where I'd been. The only time I typically paused to eat in the midst of a writing crunch was during the cycle of the full moon. I suppose that had something to do with the energy required in the metamorphosis of my human body from a six-foot-two-inch, two-hundred-pound human into a one-hundred-fifty-pound, six-foot-long gray wolf and then back again. I can only imagine the number of calories such a transmogrification requires from a person. Not to mention the calories I likely burn when I'm tearing around Central Park all night on four legs.

No, let me correct that—I don't really need to imagine the effect it has.

I know it intimately.

When I'm going through that time of the month, I'm ravenous. And I never should have considered going as long as I had today without eating.

I had to consciously force my mouth closed to keep my tongue from hanging out because the canine instinct inside me was strong with wanting to see if I could pick up more of the flavor from the similarly enhanced taste buds there.

But the smell of the place reminded me of just how incredible their food was, and it made me glad we agreed to meet here.

As I said, I hadn't seen her yet.

And I didn't know what she looked like.

I had only spoken to her on the phone when we made this date, so I didn't have a scent to go on. And with my senses muted and the poor quality of the phone connection we'd had, I hadn't picked up on her heartbeat. So I wouldn't be able to use that to single her out from among the patrons.

Standing in the front entrance and waiting for the maître d', I took in the scene. There were about twenty tables. Half of them were larger, with seating for four to six people at them, so I could rule those out. There were a few two-seater tables with pairs at them. Those were eliminated too. Only four tables had a single person at them, and only two of them were women.

One was an elderly woman I placed in her mid-sixties sitting at a table for two, wearing a stylish dark blue jacket, red horn-rimmed glasses, with long silver hair tied up in a bun at the back of her head. She was attractive, with a face that reminded me of Jessica Lange, particularly how she had looked in the promo photos for that new television show, *American Horror Story*. She also looked sharp as a handful of tacks, with an aura that didn't just say "librarian"—it screamed it in a way that would register an army of hushes from library workers across America.

Don't get me started on my lifelong immediate attraction to female librarians or, heck, any woman who spent a significant amount of time with her nose in a book.

If she was Beatrice, the woman I had spoken to on the phone last night to set up this lunch date, I knew I would likely be in for a stimulating conversation with a woman who was easy on the eye. Yep, easy on the eye and deep, meaningful conversation. The kind of afternoon that would last forever. Exactly what I needed in my life.

But not now, of course.

Because I was on a tight deadline for my latest novel.

And this wasn't a date. It was a business meeting. An arranged lunch meeting to acquire information on the occult as part of the research for my novel, *Tome of Terror*.

What the heck was wrong with me?

I mean, apart from the fact that for a full week every month, I spend my nights naked, walking around on all fours, drooling and howling at the moon. And apart from the fact that I hadn't had a significant relationship in more than ten years.

I wasn't here to spend the afternoon wining and dining a handsome woman whose conversation, I could predict, would be as stimulating as her physical appeal. I was here to get work done. Gather information, eat a delicious meal, make notes, then get back to my apartment and write all afternoon before the inevitable sunset metamorphosis.

Okay, so perhaps this lunch date *was* with her. I figured it would be an informative and entertaining afternoon. And it wouldn't hurt if I lingered a little longer for some enjoyable conversation and human interaction. What would an extra hour or so really set me back?

I turned my gaze from the Jessica Lange librarian and down several tables to the other single woman at the two-seater table farther down that row.

And my heart leaped into my throat.

A stunning brunette in her mid-twenties with a short pixie-style cut that brilliantly framed her gorgeous face, with pronounced rounded cheekbones and captivating blue eyes, was staring intently at me. It was the type of look any healthy heterosexual man could feel in his hip pocket. And it had pretty much that effect on me as our eyes locked. I shifted uncomfortably, and she smiled and nodded, mouthing my name.

"Michael?"

Even without being able to smell her over the powerful scent of the food at Antonio's or hear her distinct heartbeat or the silently mouthed word, there was no doubt that she was my date, the woman I'd spoken to on the phone.

I grinned and mouthed her name. "Beatrice?"

She nodded and smiled again, and her eyes lit up in a way that made her even more beautiful, if that was possible. I felt my mouth pulling into what must have looked like an idiotic shit-eating grin.

The maître d' arrived, walking in front of me and cutting her off from my view. It had the effect of temporarily breaking the spell Beatrice's look had on me. I actually gave my head a quick shake.

"Good afternoon, sir." He smiled, clasping his hands in front of him. He had a slight French accent—a bit off-brand for an Italian restaurant—and the way he looked and stood reminded me of Eric Idle in the role of Gaston, the French waiter in *Monty Python's The Meaning of Life*, right down to the thick cowlick and mustache. The juxtaposition of the British look and French sound reminded me of the opposite of something that had always bothered me about Captain Jean-Luc Picard on *Star Trek: The Next Generation*. Patrick Stewart, a brilliant actor, was supposed to be playing a man born in France, yet he spoke with a UK English dialect and exuded typical British behavior and habits.

"Is monsieur here with a reservation this afternoon?" he asked, clinching the nickname I'd already immediately assigned him in my head.

This Jean-Luc Idle character was close enough that I could pick up on a whiff of smugness and acknowledgment that he knew exactly what I had been transfixed by as he had arrived.

"U-uh," I stammered. "I have a reservation. It's, ah, under the name Andrews."

"Ah yes. Very good. Your lovely *young* dinner companion has arrived and is seated at your table." He sprinkled just a slight bit of extra weight into the word "young" as he spoke, subtly calling out the difference in our ages. His eyes flitted lightning-quick to the slight, still-retracting bulge in my pants that Beatrice's gaze had inspired, and I caught an additional scent of that knowing smugness. "I trust you have already seen that though, yes?"

I nodded slowly. And I'm sure my mouth might have also been hanging open. This guy was good. Perfectly polite and respectful in all manners, and yet brilliantly subtle in his condescension toward me.

"Very good. Come with me. Right this way, monsieur."

He beckoned me to follow him, which I did. As Beatrice came back into sight, her eyes were again fixed on me. They pulled me in like a sci-fi tractor beam from the aforementioned *Star Trek*. As we approached the table with Jessica Lange, I broke my eye contact with Beatrice and glanced over at the older woman I had thought might be this afternoon's dinner companion, and let out a longing sigh.

Sure, beauty, sexiness, and all that allure were still pulling me toward Beatrice, even though I wasn't looking there. It was fine. Even a little exciting. It spoke directly to my raw animal instinct. I wondered briefly if I would have the time to take her back to my place for an afternoon rendezvous before I had to make an excuse to part ways so I could howl at the moon.

But there was something even more appealing, more alluring about the woman who gave off the essence of a librarian. Jessica Lange glanced up at me, and I smiled a tight-lipped grin at her as I passed.

"Careful, Tiger," she whispered under her breath, but it was enough for me to hear. "That one will eat you alive."

And that clinched it for me. She was observant and perceptive, on top of the other traits I had inferred about her. She had intuited a great deal with just visual input.

Damn, I would have loved to marvel at the conversation we could have had, even if she wasn't the subject matter expert that I had been intending on meeting with.

When would I ever again meet another woman like that?

Jean-Luc was now blocking my view of Beatrice as I continued to follow him. But as we arrived at the table with Beatrice, she was in full view again. Her eyes were still locked on mine, fixated on me, as if we'd never broken eye contact.

She was even more ravishing up close. The heightened sexuality and desire spilling off her, which I could now smell, was overpowering.

"Michael," she said in a confident and exuberant voice as if we were long-lost friends rather than meeting for the first time.

"Good afternoon, Beatrice," I smiled as I settled into my seat. I had planned on saying it was wonderful to meet her, but that would have made her familial greeting look awkward in front of the maître d'.

Jean-Luc, his hands still clasped in front of him, leaned forward and commanded my attention as if he was about to share his life philosophy like the pseudo–Monty Python character his look reminded me of.

"Can I interest monsieur in something from the bar while you look over the menu?"

I noticed that Beatrice already had a glass of red wine in front of her.

"Oh yes," she said in a smooth and sensual breath before I could reply. "Do you have The Macallan?"

"We do, madame."

"Michael will have two fingers, served neat."

"Very well." Jean-Luc nodded.

"And a glass of club soda with lime, please," I said. I hadn't been planning on drinking this afternoon. I normally never drink on a day when I am writing. But, again, I didn't want to correct or embarrass my lunch companion.

"Anything else for madame or monsieur?"

We both shook our heads.

"I'll have them both brought over." Jean-Luc nodded his head once more before departing the table.

I watched him leave and then turned back to Beatrice. She was staring intently at me, exuding an intense passion and desire. The combination of that look and the scent transfixed and stunned me. Up close, her beauty was almost mesmerizing. I had always been intimidated by beautiful people, both men and women, so that was throwing me a bit.

I'd been about to ask her how she knew my preferred drink when she spoke.

"I'll bet the maître d' reminds you of the waiter from that Monty Python movie." She let out a little laugh that was charming and quite sensual.

"Uh," I said, pausing. "Yeah. Yeah, he did."

"I love their films," she said. "But *Life of Brian* is my absolute favorite."

"Mine too," I said. "Er, speaking of favorites, how did you know about my favorite scotch?"

"Oh," she said. "I read the interview with you in *Esquire* where you shared your adoration of Rush drummer Neil Peart. You started drinking the same brand of scotch that he preferred after reading about it in one of his travel memoirs."

"Hmm." I smiled.

"I went out and bought a bottle of that scotch to try it. But I don't like it all that much, I'm afraid. I've never really enjoyed whiskey. I'm more of a wine girl. But I also watched all of Monty Python's movies and television shows. I wasn't as fond of the TV program, but I did like the movies. *Monty Python and the Holy Grail* and *Life of Brian* were the best ones. Maybe because they are historical, which reminds me a bit of the antiquarian bookseller in your novels."

I nodded, still not saying anything. I was still uncomfortable with the fact that complete strangers knew so much about me. Having been a writer for most of my life, I had been used to the idea of living in relative poverty and obscurity.

But that had all changed in the past several years.

First came the money, which started when several of my books had been optioned by different movie and television production studios. The revenue from film and television options was a hearty chunk of money, making my book royalty numbers pale by comparison. But when the option on my novel *Print of the Predator* was greenlit into a seventy-million-dollar thriller set to feature Ryan Gosling and, within the space of about four weeks, a made-for-television film/pilot for a series was also greenlit from a different studio, the money became life-changing. Such a deal was an anomaly for a midlist author like me. My face and name started to appear in publishing industry journals and in the mass appeal entertainment magazines, newspapers, and tabloids.

The *Esquire* magazine feature she was talking about came out just last month as a tie-in for the blockbuster release coming this summer, and included photos of me on the set with Ryan Gosling, who, admittedly, looked a bit like me. A bit like me, only Gosling was far more handsome, far more sexy, far more everything. But it made sense that there would be a basic similarity between us because Gosling was cast to play Maxwell Bronte, the hero of that book series, an antiquities book dealer turned amateur detective. Bronte was, of course, based on me, or at least a fantastical version of me, with the same physical traits. Don't judge me on that. Plenty of writers do that, particularly in their first books. And Bronte was the first major novel character I'd created.

"The *Esquire* article, and a couple of the other ones about you," Beatrice continued, "also mentioned how fond you had always been of Spider-Man. I also watched all three of the Spider-Man movies starring Tobey Maguire and even found some of the comic books that I've started reading. I don't like them as much as I love your novels. I can't wait to see the movie. Maybe we can go together."

Sexy as this woman was, this was getting far too uncomfortable.

She placed her hand on the table midway between us, palm up, leaning in. The look in her eyes was clear that she intended me to put my hand onto hers, and I did. What can I say? I might be living in a boisterous, larger-than-life city that never sleeps, but I'm a polite, small-town Canadian by birth. Sure, I transplanted myself here in the early 2000s, but some manners and behaviors are so deeply ingrained that they don't disappear.

As my hand touched hers, she placed her other hand over the top of mine, enclosing my right hand between hers and gently stroking the back of my hand with her thumb. Despite the awkwardness of everything about the moment, her touch sent a delicious shiver down my spine that overrode my apprehension. It was an entirely erotic feeling, and it reminded me of how unspeakably long it had been since I'd been with a woman, never mind experienced such a sensual and intimate skin-on-skin touch.

"Oh. Michael," she breathed. "I'm so glad to finally meet you. It feels like I've known you forever."

There was an uncomfortable silence as I shifted, trying to make room for my growing erection, and at a complete loss of words for what to say in response.

Dammit, you can take the meek boy out of the small town, but Hollywood deals, fortune and fame aside, you can't take the small town out of the boy.

I took a deep breath as she beamed a radiant smile across the table at me, urging, with every fiber in my being, to focus on the cerebral, not the physical, not the animal instinct that she was compelling in me. I finally gained enough composure to speak.

"I have to admit that you have me at a loss, Beatrice," I said. "You know so much about me, but all I know about you is that you're an expert in the occult."

"Oh, that," she said, letting out a giggle, releasing my hand and then picking up her wine. "Listen, Michael, there's something I need to admit. Something I need to come clean about with you."

"Come clean?"

Just then, our waiter arrived with my scotch and glass of club soda.

"Have you both now had a chance to look at the menu?" he asked as he set the drinks down in front of me. "Would you like to hear today's specials?"

"Not yet," Beatrice replied. "Give us another five minutes."

"Of course. Take your time," he said, slipping away from our table.

Beatrice held her wineglass up. "Now that your drink has arrived, let's have a proper toast."

I looked at both glasses. I hadn't planned on drinking, but everything about this moment was completely overwhelming. I grabbed the scotch glass.

"A toast," she said, clinking her glass against my tumbler. "To us. To this magical moment. And to the beginning of something truly special."

I nodded, again at a loss for words.

Yes, I was flattered. Yes, I was turned on by this gorgeous woman. What healthy man wouldn't bask in this fawning attention? But it was all so sudden and far too rushed. And completely inappropriate. I'd decided, long ago, that I should do my best to avoid physical intimacy. Just in case.

We were supposed to be meeting so she could share research that I could use in my latest novel. My agent's assistant, Anne, had set this meeting up. I wondered if Anne, who normally would never do such a thing, might have tricked me and tried to use this business meeting as a ruse to set me up with a fan. She knew I was single, and had been since I'd known her and her boss.

But what Anne didn't know was that part of the reason I hadn't had any sort of intimate relationship with a woman was because of my werewolf affliction. How could I actually be with anyone when, for almost a full week every month, I turned into a four-legged predatory canine?

I had never been a charmer. Prior to gaining the extrasensory ability to read people's intentions through their scent and their heartbeat, I was never that good at picking up on cues that a woman was into me. But even if I hadn't had supernatural senses, there was no disputing the fact that this woman was beyond just being "into me." There was no doubt that sex wasn't just on the table. It was under the table, on the floor, on the counter, in the hallway, up against the wall, wherever and however many times I wanted.

That certainly appealed to the underlying animal instinct in me. But it made me extremely uncomfortable. Because her obsession and desire for me were unhealthy. I couldn't take advantage of this poor woman's own affliction.

Even if this wasn't such a bizarro-world moment for me, I wasn't ready to again try being intimate with a woman.

I needed to change the subject and get this back on track to why I was here.

"Before," I said and my voice cracked on the second syllable. I cleared my throat and started again. "Before the waiter arrived, you said something about coming clean."

"Ah yes. I was."

"What was it?"

"Well," she said, "I told that nice secretary I had been talking to that I was an expert in the occult."

"And?"

"And I actually don't know anything about the occult. All I know is that I wanted to meet you. I *needed* to meet you, Michael. So, I lied to her about my background. Just for the chance to get to meet you in person."

"Uh, I'm not sure..." I said, putting my scotch glass back down and then picking up the soda and taking a drink before speaking, partially so I could come up with the words to let her down without being rude about it. *How the hell do Hollywood stars deal with this type of thing on an ongoing basis?* "I'm not sure that having lunch is a good idea."

I had been anticipating her response as a scent of disappointment and despair. But I didn't get that at all. Instead, I heard her heart skip a beat and got a whiff of excited anticipation.

"Oh Michael, I never expected you to be so forward. But of course I'm into that. I'm so into you. Let's skip lunch. Let's finish these drinks so we can get out of here and," she paused ever so briefly, tilted her head toward me and gave me an exaggerated wink, "get to really know each other better."

I had never had a woman proposition me like that before. At least not that obviously and blatantly.

"Uh," was all I managed to say.

I hadn't been expecting that.

"I can't wait to show you just how into you I am," she purred. "I can't wait to see just how into *me* you can get." She delivered that last line with another wink. "I mean, I saw that bulge in your pants when you approached the table. I've got multiple places we can put it."

I took a second and glanced over my shoulder to see if there were hidden cameras around and if I had blundered my way into one of those *Candid Camera* or *Punk'd* shows. It was, of course, a delay tactic. I had no idea what to do, but I could tell by her scent that Beatrice was genuinely propositioning me. This wasn't a prank.

To be completely honest, a part of me was actually tempted, on a level far removed from possibility. The way you might contemplate, ever so briefly, picking up a live wire or pushing your palm onto the glowing red-hot element of a stove. She was one of the most beautiful women I'd ever encountered, and she was into me, no question about it. I was a healthy heterosexual man who hadn't been intimate with a woman in...well, let's not get into how long it had been because I'd have to take my shoes and socks off if I wanted to count that high.

Even if this didn't work out relationship-wise, I suspected it would be an incredible night that I would never forget.

But it wasn't right.

And on top of that, if what some might see as my prudish response wasn't enough, I hadn't planned on spending the afternoon rolling in the sheets but rather rolling page after page through my typewriter to make progress toward my novel's deadline.

If anything, I felt a little bit sorry for Beatrice.

Here was a beautiful woman. She was articulate and intelligent. From all external perspectives—I really didn't know anything about her—she seemed to have a lot going on. She could likely have virtually any man she wanted. But she was practically throwing herself at my feet.

Like I said, it just wasn't right.

She thought she was into me. But she wasn't. She was into my celebrity, this temporary moment of fame I found myself basking in—having movie and television deals made from my novels, cresting the waves of the *New York Times* bestseller list, appearing in magazines like *Esquire* and *Men's Journal,* and spotted on set with actors like Ryan Gosling and Rachel McAdams. She was into the allure of my current status.

Was this what movie stars and rock stars felt like? Never being able to just have a real interaction with people as a person, always as an icon. How did they get used to it? How did they get past that initial fascination and form real relationships?

Yeah, I know: it sounds like I'm full of myself.

But you've got to remember, I can see through the surface lies and masks that people put up for the world, and understand a bit more about the hidden intent behind a person's words or actions via their scent. While I've used it to my advantage in negotiations for my career, I have tried not to use it to personally take advantage of people, especially folks like Beatrice.

I could tell that Beatrice would be fine if all we did was go and have wild and passionate sex. She was fine with being used, because she was fine with using me at the same time. It would be a mutual benefit experience. I doubted she was looking for a long-term relationship, which was something I couldn't have anyway. She was looking for a fling with a "name" and a kiss-and-tell story she could share with her social circles for years.

As turned on as I was by the visual beauty I beheld across the table, the whole thought of it turned me off. Heck, when I'd walked in here, I'd been ravenous and practically drooling at the smell of food. And when I'd first seen this woman, I'd immediately felt a more animal hunger. But both of those cravings had faded away.

"Uh," I said again. It's a good thing I enjoy striking keys and laying words down on the page because apparently I'm not all that good at forming them into coherent sentences past my lips.

"There is, of course," she said, "only one question now."

"Um, what's that?"

"My place or yours?"

I picked up the soda glass again and drank it down, trying to buy some time to figure out how to explain that she had misunderstood my intent.

But I knew I was just avoiding the inevitable—trying to let this woman down as gently as possible.

And likely spending the rest of the daylight hours sitting in my apartment alone in front of a keyboard and a blank page, wondering what the hell was wrong with me, all the while waiting for the secret society of manly men to take away my man card.

Chapter Two

GAIL

"Mine's bigger than yours," I panted.

"Your what?"

"My man card. It's bigger than yours."

He flipped me off, but I just laughed and pushed harder. Hot, sticky sweat dripped down my face. I leaned forward. The rhythm was intoxicating, the strain of my muscles both painful and exhilarating.

"Fuck, yes," I moaned, hearing my voice waver. I took another deep breath. "Faster!" It came out as a whisper as I pushed harder. "Almost there!"

I forced all my energy into my legs and pumped my arms. All I could hear was the sound of my sneakers hitting the pavement. Sweat ran into my eyes, and I could barely see my destination, but I knew that the stairs leading down to Gansevoort Street signaled the southern end of the High Line.

I pressed on, reached the stairs, and bounded down them two at a time.

"Yes!"

I hit the concrete at the bottom, stopped the timer on my watch, and put my hands up over my head, Rockystyle, to celebrate my victory. When Benjamin caught up to me, I was still dancing.

He stopped when he reached me and bent over, hands on his knees, to catch his breath.

"You okay there, pal?" I asked, slapping his back a little harder than I needed to.

He stood up, his face flushed, and glared at me. "What did that even mean?"

"What did what mean?"

"That thing about my man card."

"I said mine's bigger than yours."

He sniffed. "That's so unladylike."

I pretended to consider that remark. "Suck my dick," I replied.

Ben did not laugh. "Jesus, Gail." He started walking away from me, and I followed, laughing.

"What's wrong? Don't like it when a girl beats you?"

"Why does everything have to be like this with you?"

I opened my mouth in a hot retort but stopped when I saw the look on his face. Normally we love to tease each other, but my brother was clearly not in the mood today. "Everything isn't like this. Whatever *this* means. I thought we were just having some fun."

"We were having fun until it became a contest. That's how you are about everything. If you can't win physically, you have to get in the last word. If you can't get the last word, you make sure you get the meanest word."

Whoa.

"Ben, what the hell? This is our thing. We tease each other."

"I just wanted to hang out with you. Have a conversation. You had to turn it into an Olympic event."

"Olympic event? Please." I stayed quiet for a second but then couldn't help myself. "I could kick those bitch-boys' asses."

He glared at me and then walked away.

"Ben!" I said. "Come on! I'm just trying to make you laugh."

"Not everything is a competition, Gail," he shouted. "I don't want to fight you. I want to talk!"

People were staring at us, but I didn't care. I've seen way worse on New York City streets.

"Then let's talk," I called back. He was far enough away that I had to yell now. But he didn't even turn around. Just raised one hand over his head in dismissal.

Ben had always been my partner in crime, the only reason I knew how to stick up for myself in the first place. He taught me the art of the street fight when I should have been playing with baby dolls. But something was wrong today. I glanced at my watch. I should have gone after him and apologized, but I knew I would barely make it to the shop on time as it was.

Call me when you can talk, I texted him. I put my phone in the pocket of my leggings and then fished it out again. **And I'm sorry.**

I didn't exactly know what I was sorry for, but it would have to do for now.

I crossed Washington Street and grabbed a smoothie from my favorite bodega. I continued east, enjoying the afternoon sunshine. Even a fight with my brother couldn't ruin a post-run high. He of all people should know that I needed the adrenaline kick. He knew what I'd been going through lately. He knew all the stress I felt from running the shop. If I didn't get this energy out of my system, my brain would explode all over the first customer of my shift. Not a good way to own a business.

Still, the nagging feeling that I'd screwed up was creeping into my endorphin rush. Maybe I should go after him?

"Family first!" I could practically hear Mom saying it now, just like she'd said it every day of our lives. As if she repeated a clichéd slogan enough times, it would make up for her absolute lack of parenting.

I didn't buy into most of what my mother had said over the years. All of her *blood is thicker than water* bullshit. I'd choose most of my girlfriends over my blood relatives any day of the week. That's what happens when you're raised in a family of crazy old bats who are one turban away from Grey Gardens. My poor brother was the lone boy in our clan, and he'd been doted on until he was practically smothered. The only attention I ever got was when I screwed up. *How is a girl who's always in trouble going to take care of her brother, Gail?*

I stopped walking. That man card crack wasn't cool. Ben was the only blood relative I actually cared about, and instead of being there for him, I'd been too consumed by my own needs. Screw work; I had to go after my brother. Family first!

I turned quickly and went after him. I knew Ben would walk all the way back to his place. But my stomach dropped when I saw a familiar figure ahead of me.

My boyfriend, Jonathan, stepped out of a brownstone.

Jonathan didn't live in this area. He lived in Brooklyn. And he was supposed to be at work right now. He'd told me he had to work all weekend to get caught up on a backlog with an important client.

I could have easily caught up to him, but I remained rooted in my spot, dread filling my gut.

Maybe it wasn't him. Maybe it was his doppelgänger. I read once that every human has six identical lookalikes around the world. If I was ever going to see one of Jonathan's lookalikes, it would be here in Manhattan. Half the men in this city looked like him. This man was the same height, wore an identical gray business suit, and walked with the same little hitch in his right leg that Jonathan had.

Maybe he was coming to surprise me? He was headed in the wrong direction.

Maybe he was going to buy flowers? But why had he stopped at this random house?

Just a few steps behind him, a gorgeous blonde woman came through the same door. Their body language was easy enough to read, even from this distance. Jonathan placed his hand on the small of her back, and she smiled up at him.

The gulp of smoothie I'd just taken turned to cement in my mouth, and I had to swallow hard to get it down. I knew this feeling well.

Far too well.

When you've been cheated on as many times as I have been, an instinct kicks in, a knowledge of an all too familiar feeling. Each time I dated someone new, I hoped I was rid of that cynicism. And each time, it returned like an irritating rash.

"You're overreacting," I muttered to myself, between deep breaths. "It's probably nothing."

Someday, it would be nothing. Someday I'd meet a man, think he was up to something sketchy, and be wrong about it. It would be a sister, a cousin, or a work colleague. I couldn't wait for the day when my suspicions were unfounded.

But I followed him anyway.

They walked a few blocks south and headed into a diner. If his hand on her back didn't tell me what I needed to know, the way she wiggled her ass and bumped her hip into his did. Cousins don't walk together like that.

Part of my brain still refused to see what was right in front of me. If my eyes weren't deceiving me, that would make Jonathan the third cheater in a row. What does that tell you about my judgment in men?

I was so close to turning around and walking away. I could have continued on my path back to my apartment, where I would take a shower, grab a sandwich, and take over the evening shift at the shop. When I called Jonathan later, he would have told me that he stayed up late last night working on actuarial tables or whatever the hell it is that finance bros do with their time. It would have been a lie, but I could have lived with that lie for a little while longer. At that moment, I so wished I was the type of woman who could live in ignorant bliss. Maybe people who turn away from their partner's bullshit are happier overall.

Unfortunately, I am not that woman. Maybe Ben was right about my need to win all the time.

They sat down three tables back, holding hands across the table, laughing about something. She was so blonde and so, so young. I placed her in her early twenties. Unblemished, smooth white skin, high cheekbones, taut breasts, slim, boyish hips. I took my focus off them and caught my own reflection in the window. At thirty-five, I wasn't exactly old, but I was definitely disheveled. My hair had fallen out of the loose bun I'd worn that morning, and sweat had caked the strands onto my neck. My face was mottled and red from the exertion of running, and I didn't need to duck my nose into my shirt to know I smelled horrible.

I could have taken the dignified route here. I could have called him, left a voice message, told him calmly that we were over and he should pick up all of his shit from my place. I could have sent a letter. I could have pretended I didn't see anything.

But I didn't.

A strange confidence overtook me, and I recognized it. It was the same feeling I'd had when I'd seen Ben a few steps ahead of me on our run.

I had to win.

I strode into the diner. Jonathan was facing the door, like the douche canoe that he is. What kind of man doesn't even try to hide? When he saw me, he yanked his hands out of hers, knocking a water glass over.

"Gail!" he said. "I can explain!"

"No, you really can't," I said. I slowly removed the lid and straw from my cup, extended my arm, and dumped the smoothie over his head.

Turning on one heel, I walked out of the diner slowly, as if I didn't even notice the sputtering and cursing mess behind me. Not only had I ruined his stupid business suit, but he was probably about to have a tense conversation with the Barbie doll.

As for me, I was free of him.

But when I stepped out of the diner and resumed my walk home, I had to fight back tears. That was the thing about winning: it was never as satisfying as I thought it would be.

Sunday, May 22, 2011

Chapter Three

MICHAEL
10:03 a.m.

I had to fight back tears of frustration and anger as I stared at the blank page of the Word document in front of me.

I thought it would be different.

But after all these years of wins in my writing life, writer's block could hit me out of the blue.

And take me back down into the darkness.

This was the wrong time.

I was already behind on the manuscript deadline, because of the time lost to the monthly cycle of morphing into a wolf from sundown to sunrise. Yesterday when I got home, I should have used that time to write.

But I didn't write a single word.

Instead, I'd spent most of the day kicking myself for turning down that blatant offer of no-strings sex from Beatrice.

It was a useless waste of time.

And now I sat here, staring at the blank page.

I tried something that sometimes kick-started the words and fueled my imagination: I typed out exactly what I'd been thinking.

Maxwell Bronte stared in glassy-eyed defiance at the blank page in front of him.

It did nothing for me except, perhaps, remind me that the line was a little derivative of the Rush song, "Losing It."

I deleted those words, then sat back in my chair and sighed.

I thumbed back from the blank chapter I'd been sitting in front of for the past half hour and scrolled through the nearly seventy thousand words I had already written in the manuscript for *Tome of Terror*.

It was the Maxwell Bronte novel where he was trying to solve a crime related to a rare edition of the *Necronomicon*. I had done enough research to fill the book with realistic enough elements. But I hadn't written—or even figured out—the climax. So, I was at that critical part of my process where I preferred to be able to bounce the existing manuscript off an expert in the field.

Something about that exercise, about the three-dimensionality of it, drove things home for me. Talking through the plot elements, the supporting characters, understanding just a little more about their world, would often give me just the right insight—some aspect that often comes in the midst of the conversation—that drives everything home for me. I suppose it's like one of the last few pieces of a jigsaw puzzle that will fit into place.

In this case, I needed an expert on the occult. And yesterday's attempt to meet with one had been a complete bust.

Not to mention embarrassing.

I hated having to turn down Beatrice. To let her down. But even if I had succumbed to the temptation of enjoying an afternoon of carnal bliss with her, I'm pretty sure when we got back to my apartment I likely would have resorted to the Poindexter I've been my whole life. I would have grinned bashfully, laughing like Goofy and saying something like, "Garsh, I think yer real pretty, but I have a book to go work on. Ayuh."

The phone on my desk rang. I picked it up.

Any distracting port in a writer's-block storm.

"Michael!" It was Anne, my agent Mack's assistant. "I'm so sorry."

She was responding to the voicemail I had left her about the off encounter I'd had with Beatrice. A connection that Anne had set up.

"I had no idea," she continued. "When she contacted us she positioned herself as an expert and outright lied about her background."

"That's okay, Anne. I know you're doing your best. Heck, in helping me with this, you're already going above and beyond."

I thought about this. Anne's role as my literary agent's personal and professional assistant meant catering to his every whim, need, and desire. And he was a demanding and belligerent boss.

Yet, despite all that Anne did for Mack, she always went out of her way to offer me additional support. She always took pity on me and provided assistance that benefited me and my writing goals.

When she'd learned I was behind with this manuscript deadline, she'd offered to spend the time sourcing an expert contact for me, knowing I needed that extra time to focus on writing and getting the manuscript completed.

"It's my pleasure, Michael," Anne said. "But I didn't just call to apologize. I called to let you know some good news."

"What's that?" I asked, hoping it would be another extension on the manuscript deadline.

"I've gotten in contact with another professional."

"Do you think that's a good idea? I'm really behind here, Anne. Yesterday's...er...misunderstanding set me back an entire day of word count. I can't afford more of that."

"This one I double-checked. She is legit. She owns an occult shop in the East Village called Enchanting Magic. Her name is Gail Sommers."

"You sure this isn't another stalker?"

"I spoke with her, Michael. Even asked her a few details about her business and about the occult. She's who and what she says she is."

I thought about it. I wasn't getting any writing done. Nothing I usually used to break out of writer's block was working. And I could do it this evening, since my cycle was finished for the month.

"Okay," I said. "I suppose it won't hurt to give this a try. Thanks, Anne. When can I meet with her?"

"I'll give you her number, and you can set something up."

*　*　*

5:55 p.m.

I glanced at the time as I reached the Barnes & Noble located at 555 Fifth Avenue. My phone was showing five fifty-five.

That coincidental juxtaposition of those things lining up brought an extra bounce to my step.

But so did the fact we'd be meeting at the Starbucks inside a magnificent bookstore. Because even if this meeting turned out to be a bust, at least I'd be able to salvage some good from it by browsing through the stacks of books.

Gail and I had chatted briefly on the phone after I'd called her. We had agreed to meet at this particular location because it was convenient for me, and she had already been planning on being in the neighborhood shortly before six p.m.

I liked it when plans fell together in that way.

But more than that, I was appreciative she'd been able to meet me today. I was already behind the eight ball with this deadline, blocked from making any progress, and I hoped that hearing some insights from a person who understood the occult and even ran a shop specializing in magic and witchcraft could kick-start what I needed to act on.

After moving through the main door and pausing to take in the powerful essence of the smell of all those books, merged with the odors of the Starbucks—a truly exquisite wonder—I turned right and walked toward the wide, open café area.

I spotted her immediately.

She was a gorgeous brunette in a black cotton shirt with a lacy frill pattern around the neck, underneath a shiny black leather jacket. Just above the neckline of the blouse, she wore a black leather collar with silver studs. Her legs were crossed under the small round table, and I could see she was wearing tight black leather pants.

This look screamed occult to me, so I was sure it had to be her.

And, intriguing as she already was in appearance, there was an additional underlying essence I picked up from her almost immediately. It hung over her like an aura, one that perhaps someone with my enhanced sensory abilities could pick up on.

She wasn't just sitting there in the café; she was subtly scoping it out—reading the room. She wasn't merely aware of all of the people around her; she was actively participating in the room's flow, its very essence.

There was a confidence and forceful feminine presence coming from the room. I knew it was her smell because of its mixture with the leather she was wearing.

She was both predatory and protective in her subtle yet powerfully mature presence over the room.

Did I mention that she was stunning? One of the most beautiful women I'd ever seen in my life?

The two or three seconds I'd had observing her felt like an hour of me standing there in awe, and I consciously checked myself to ensure my bottom jaw wasn't hanging open.

Her eyes landed on me. By the way I could hear her heart subtly change its beat, she knew exactly who I was before her lips turned up in a slight grin.

Both the look on her face and the scent coming off her were filled with the confident recognition that comes with the acknowledgment that we both knew who the other person was.

Of course, when she turned her smile at me, there was a sparkle that I can only describe as magic, coming from those green eyes that made my own heart skip a beat.

I felt as if a spell had been cast on me, and another eternity took place as I looked at her even though I knew it had only been a fraction of a second.

To have someone like her smile like that while looking me straight in the eyes was a wonder I had never known was possible.

When that eternal split second was over, I glanced down, almost certain I would spot the chin of my open mouth resting on the tops of my shoes.

I was thankful there was a purposeful intent to this meeting, otherwise I would never have had the courage to speak with such a stunning beauty.

You're here for information about the occult, I reminded myself. *This isn't a date.*

And with that reminder, I mustered up the courage to place one foot in front of the other to maneuver myself over to the table where she sat, introduce myself and get on with the business at hand.

Chapter Four

GAIL

GTG.

I sent the message and then tried to arrange my face into a Serious Businesswoman mask. Michael Andrews was coming to me for professional help.

I glanced down to shut my phone off and saw that it was flooded with messages.

GTG? What does that mean?

Gail, what is GTG?

Why aren't you replying anymore? I don't know what to do about the bees.

I quickly typed out a reply.

GTG = Got to go. In a meeting. Will call you in an hour.

Isabeau was not going to be happy with that reply, but I didn't have any options. Michael had reached my table while I was texting her. He startled me when I looked up—how did he move that fast?

"Gail?" he asked with a smile.

Holy hell.

I swallowed hard. *This is a business meeting.*

"You must be Michael. Nice to meet you."

He sat down across from me, and I snapped my phone off and dropped it in my purse. He needed my expertise. No need to act like a teenager who'd just met the lead singer of a boy band just because he was good-looking. I reminded myself again that this was a business meeting.

The sentence kept rolling through my head, like a mantra, except it wasn't registering. Nothing much was registering except that I was sitting across from this hunk of a human, and I couldn't even remember why.

"I appreciate you meeting on such short notice. I'm in a bit of a bind. I suppose Anne already told you the whole story?"

"N-not much. Some of it. You need my help for a book you're writing?"

"Sort of," he replied, and then he did that thing that men do when they want to kill you right on the spot. While he talked, he took off his jacket, draped it over his seat, unbuttoned his cuffs, and rolled his sleeves up to his elbows. Right there at the Starbucks table, like an assassin.

How was I supposed to concentrate? He had forearms like Popeye, for Chrissake. I considered calling the police.

"Do you think you can help me?"

I blinked at him. I hadn't heard a word he'd said.

"Yes," I replied. Because obviously that's what you do when an attractive assassin asks you for professional help. You say yes, even if you have absolutely no clue what they need.

"All of it?" he asked. "Even back to the sixteen hundreds?"

I stared for a moment. "What's in the sixteen hundreds?" I asked stupidly.

He sighed, and his dark eyebrows furrowed. His appreciation of my expertise was waning, undoubtedly because I was behaving like a total moron. I took a deep breath and shook my head a little bit. My ability to get distracted by men's forearms notwithstanding, I had a job to do.

"It's loud in here," I said. "I missed that last part. Tell me what you need again?"

"Well, I'm mostly looking for some more esoteric understanding about occultism in relation to Christianity through the years. In particular, how religious leaders have weaponized it against nondominant cultures for their own gain. And what ties the fictional text of the *Necronomicon* may play a role in any of this. I have a few books—"

At this point, he whipped out his own phone and held up a list of book titles for me to examine. A lot of the basic texts on mysticism, with a few outliers sprinkled in there for good measure. He'd probably just gone down the line on the Amazon bestseller list.

"Oh, you've got a great start," I said. "These are the standards. You'll learn pretty much everything you need to know with these."

"Well, obviously not," he said slowly. "Or I wouldn't be asking for help."

"What more do you need?"

"Every one of these books tells me this event happened this year, and this person wrote a book about it. I'm more interested in the development of the beliefs and the tension of the dominant society of the time."

"Understand the people and you'll understand the stories."

He nodded, just slightly, and the left corner of his mouth went up.

Pagan gods above, I do love a man who knows how to wield a smirk.

"That's right," he said thoughtfully. "That's right. I am a writer of stories."

I felt my body temperature go up a solid five degrees and shifted in my seat. Leather pants had seemed like a great idea when I left the house, but I didn't know I'd be having a conversation with a man whose eyes actually smoldered. I had the strangest sensation that he could tell I was sweating because he narrowed his eyes just a bit and almost seemed to be enjoying my discomfort.

"You're not what I expect a writer to look like," I blurted out.

His smirk deepened, and he sat back and crossed his legs at the ankles. What was this guy—eight feet, nine feet tall? His legs practically reached across Fifth Avenue.

"You're not what I expect an occult shop owner to look like."

Well, touché. One backhanded compliment deserved another. I should probably redirect the conversation before he decided to tell me that one time in college, he dated a girl who looked just like Stevie Nicks.

Before I could speak, he stood from the table. "I need a coffee. What can I get you?"

"Nothing. You go first. I'll get mine next. Don't want to lose our table. This is prime real estate."

He walked over to the counter, and I had to physically restrain myself from turning in my seat to watch him go.

I reached for my phone as discreetly as I could.

Isabeau had blown up my phone in the ten minutes since I'd last texted her.

What meeting?
Is it animal control?
I don't know what to do with this guy.
He's asking about the lease.
Honey is dripping out of the electrical sockets!
Gail, I think you need to talk to this guy.
Gail??

Michael returned to the table just as I stood up and put the phone to my ear.

"Excuse me for one minute," I said to him with the most unconcerned smile I could manage. "My business partner needs my help with a bee situation."

He shrugged and sat down.

I moved to get into the huge line that had accumulated at the counter.

"What is going on?" I asked when Isabeau picked up the phone.

"To get to the beehive, they have to rip out a wall. The estimate is a huge, scary number, G. Plus, they want to spray a bunch of pesticides in there."

"No pesticides," I say firmly. "That's nonnegotiable. Where is Len?" Our reptilian landlord was supposed to be handling all this. I rubbed the space between my eyebrows, trying to ward off a quickly approaching cluster headache.

"He's here. Fighting me about the cost. Blaming us for the bees. As if we have control over nature!"

Deep breath, Gail.

"Well, that's nonsense. We have insurance. Len has insurance. They don't need to rip out walls; I'm sure someone can get to it through the attic. We'll fight this."

"Yes, I understand that in the long run we'll be okay. But that's going to take time, and we've got to figure out how to replace the damaged merchandise, or we won't have customers."

"Well, the good news is I'm across town doing some consulting work for this guy. A writer. His agent called me early this morning and offered me five thousand dollars for some research help. Evidently, he's pretty big-time. I was just thinking I should leave, but I'll stay. We need this money."

"A writer?" she asked. "Is he weird?"

"No!" I said, perhaps a bit too loudly. "Why would you think that?"

"Dunno," she replied. I could imagine her nonchalant shrug, her birdlike shoulders pushing the black spirals of her hair out of the way. "In the movies, writers always look a little hungover. Why were you just about to leave?"

"This one doesn't look hungover. He's—" I glanced over at Michael. He didn't have his phone out, he hadn't grabbed a book or magazine, he didn't have a laptop or a notebook. He was just sitting there, sipping his coffee, like some kind of psychopath.

"He's what?" Isabeau prompted.

Michael had been gazing at the couple at the table next to ours, but they stood up to leave so his gaze shifted around the room. I watched his eyes travel from person to person, lingering every now and then, tilting his head while he observed. Occasionally he sipped his coffee, but he never stopped watching. There was something endearing about his curiosity.

"He's nice," I finally responded. "He seems like a really nice guy."

There was a pause. "How tall is he?"

"Isabeau—"

"Oh, hell no!"

"Isabeau!"

"I said *hell* no. Do you hear me, Gail? Absolutely hell to the damn no!"

"It's not what you think."

"What is it, then?" she challenged.

"I'm *working*."

"Then tell me what he looks like."

I sighed. "Nothing. Just a regular guy."

She paused before she replied, and when she spoke, her voice was pitched scary low. "I'm going to say this once, Gail Sommers. *Once.* You get the hell out of that place. Right. This. Second."

"I can't just leave. This is supposed to be a business consultation."

"And you are supposed to be celibate for a year. Do you remember that? Do you remember crying on my couch? Do you remember setting all of Jonathan's clothes on fire in Tompkins Square Park just yesterday afternoon and that fine you got from the fire department? Do you remember how you vowed to do all that self-improvement bullshit?"

"I went to a yoga class this morning," I said, rather vaguely. Then I addressed the barista, who was waiting to take my order. "One venti Pike Place, please."

"You need to walk out of that room," Isabeau replied. "Tell him you can't help him, and he needs to find someone else. Tell him to make up occult stuff because that's what writers do. They lie. That's literally their job, even the tall ones! Or, just tell him to go to one of the million other occult shop owners in New York."

I handed over some cash, not at all sure my credit card would be accepted. "But I'm the only one with a beehive in her store and an intense need for a revenge fuck." I knew she'd flip out the second I said that last part, but sometimes I can't help teasing her.

"One year of celibacy!" she sputtered. "You promised me! How else will you learn whatever you're supposed to be learning this year?"

I wanted to laugh, but I also needed to extricate myself from this conversation. Any minute now, Michael would decide I was a flake and walk out of the café. Besides the fact that I wanted to stare into his Marlon Brando eyes for a while longer, I really needed that money.

"Isabeau, listen to me. Take a breath. This is a whole new Gail. I took this job because we need the cash. I can still notice good-looking men, even when I'm celibate. I'm at a coffee-slash-work appointment. That's it. Now, if there is nothing else, I'm going to get back to my meeting."

Silence met me from the other end of the phone. I waited for a few beats. She didn't answer, but I knew she was still there. I could hear her breathing and doing that tap-tappy thing she did with her fingernails when she was pissed.

"Iz," I said, taking the coffee they'd poured for me over to the cream and sugar table. I normally drank it black but needed to delay getting back to Michael for another minute. "This here, what you are doing? This is the divine feminine in action. Women looking out for each other, using their power to uplift and support each other, channeling their rage for good." I paused, trying to think of more keywords that would calm her down. Bringing up feminine spirituality was always a good idea when Isabeau was fed up with me. "I receive your positive energy, and I'm grateful for you. Okay? Now, let me get distracted by this handsome-but-off-limits-to-me hunk of burning manhood. I promise all of my clothes will remain on my body. Okay?"

Finally, I heard a long sigh. "I don't know, G. I'm just not sure if I can trust you," she said. "Exactly how tall is he?"

I bit back a laugh. One thing about Isabeau, she took her job as my best friend seriously. At the very least I was in for a long lecture. At worst, she'd show up to this café with a chastity belt for me and some large, pointy crystals, which she would fling into Michael's unusually handsome head.

"He's not that tall. And I love you more than oxygen. I'll be back at the shop in a couple of hours. Deal?"

Michael's coffee was empty when I got back to the table, and I apologized for disappearing for so long.

"It's not a problem," he said. "Watching people is an important part of my job."

"Is that where you get ideas for your books?"

"Sometimes," he said with a slightly abashed shrug. "I like to eavesdrop. That was an intense conversation you were having."

"You could hear that?" This strange and sexy writer must have the ears of a fruit bat. I hoped he hadn't caught the word *celibate*.

"Body language, mostly," he said. "An argument?"

I sighed. "Our store is infested with bees." I corrected myself when I saw the look of alarm on his face. "Well, not infested. Not exactly. We had noticed a few bees milling around, and then this morning, there was honey dripping out of the ceiling fixtures."

Even though his face looked placid, I had the strangest sensation that he knew I wasn't telling the whole truth about my conversation.

"It's not as unusual as you might think," I continued, even though I realized how absolutely bananas I sounded. "Beehives can be huge. Something happened to damage their hive—a rodent of some sort, most likely—and the hive broke, and the honey is seeping out."

"Out of the walls?" he looked confused.

"Well, it drips down the walls and pools on the ground. It smells delicious."

"Can you eat it?"

I shrugged. "I mean, there are probably a lot of toxins in the building. Then again, supposedly honey is antibacterial."

"I think I'd try it," he says. "Imagine, you could just wipe your toast along the wall every morning, and breakfast is ready."

I laughed out loud at this, but the mention of food got my stomach growling. "Do you want to go next door and get some dinner? We can talk there. I'm a lot more coherent when I get a little pasta in me."

He didn't answer right away. He assessed me with his head cocked to one side. The way he looked at me made me feel exposed, and I noticed my hand nervously checking the buttons on my shirt. The smirk returned, and my heart rate sped up again.

The problem was, New Gail didn't make out with tall strangers. New Gail meditated and got acupuncture and sent good vibes to the world. New Gail didn't have time for people as common as men because she was too busy being spiritually divine and astrally calm and wonderfully single and sacredly celibate.

"That sounds great," he said. "I'm starving."

Old Gail would have suggested we grab a cab back to her place and have him half undressed before making it up the stairs.

Chapter Five

MICHAEL
6:35 p.m.

I was glad the place we were going was right next door and that we didn't have to hail a cab or anything like that to get there.

Because until Gail mentioned it, I hadn't realized just how hungry I was.

"I'm starving," I repeated, getting up from the table and plucking my jacket from the back of my chair.

As we moved out of the café and to the escalator, I was reminded of the hunger pangs I'd felt walking into Antonio's Urban Kitchen yesterday. I had been tantalized by the smell of the food there, but I'd also been tempted by the offer the hot young Beatrice had made.

Heck, I'd felt the heat radiating off Beatrice immediately. Her scent and the looks she'd given me had resonated immediately in my groin.

Yesterday, of course, I didn't enjoy a bite of the delicious meal across from a beautiful young woman. The taste of the food was off, and the meal seemed to last forever. Because I was too nervous about how to politely reject the pretty fan's blatant advances. And every single moment that passed had come with an agonizing desire for me to finish that meal, get out of there, and remove myself from the situation.

Completely unlike how I felt tonight.

Gail was closer to my age, near pushing forty, and an absolutely stunning beauty. Sure, she was pleasing to the eye, the type of beauty you feel good about just looking at. But what I loved about her was she was dynamic and multi-layered.

That made her far more beautiful, far more appealing to me.

And though I picked up an intense sexual desire off of Gail within a split second of my first word to her, there was something far deeper at play, I could sense.

While I could tell, from the emotive scent she gave off and how her heartbeat reacted to things I said and did, that she was really into me.

As into me as I was into her.

She thought I was hot. But that's not what appealed to me. That's not what intrigued me. No, it was those layers. It was the fact she kept repressing it, or at least trying to repress it, and hiding that desire behind layers. That was what intrigued me.

Because it felt like her desire for me was playing peekaboo. The "now here" and "now gone" aspect was so bloody appealing, and it drew me into her even further.

She was also completely aware of her surroundings while appearing oblivious to them. Though she was subtle about it, I could tell she was aware of the position and actions of everyone in that café. And I was curious to know what it was that led her to be.

I have enhanced senses; I can hear, see, and smell things the average person isn't aware of. But Gail seemed to have some sort of dynamic ability to perceive the room in a way she very carefully didn't let on to anyone else around her. I'm not even sure she was aware of it.

When she'd taken that call from her female friend, I consciously focused on not listening in. I'd been able to hear every word Gail said, and every word her friend Isabeau said.

It was something about bees and attics and ruined merchandise.

But it was none of my business.

I did my best to focus on other noises and sounds around me. If I attend to something specific, I can drown out the other static noises. I tried paying attention to the conversation between an elderly couple at the far side of the bar. They'd been squabbling about the deadbeat boyfriend of their forty-year-old daughter, who still lived in their basement.

This worked, keeping me from listening in on much of Gail's conversation.

Only short snippets of what Gail was saying made it to me, and I did my best to ignore them.

But I couldn't ignore two of the things I heard.

Five thousand dollars and *celibacy*.

The first one had been uttered by Gail. I wondered if that was the cost of whatever insect incident they'd been speaking about came to.

As for celibacy, that had come from Isabeau. And I had no idea what the context was, nor how it related to their beehive mishap.

Isabeau was hot for the beekeeper, who was a celibate.

I was hot for Gail.

I gestured for her to enter the revolving doors exiting the Barnes & Noble first. I took that brief moment to enjoy a quick look at her very fine ass in those tight black leather pants as she moved ahead of me.

I'd heard the expression *the kind of ass you could bounce a quarter off of* before, but until just then, it had never made any sense to me.

"Tommy Bahama right next door is more known for its seafood," I said when we reconvened together outside on the sidewalk. "They have great food but aren't known for their pasta. And we might not get a table right away without a reservation."

That wasn't entirely true. I'm sure I would be able to get us in by playing the Mack Halpin card. My literary agent carried a lot of sway in this city, and I had occasionally used it to bypass the regular lines at some establishments.

But I didn't want to be showing off. I wanted, instead, to be using this time to focus on what Gail could teach me about the occult. And, if I were to be completely honest, to enjoy focusing on those gorgeous green eyes as long as possible.

"That was just an expression," she said. "Like saying *I'm so hungry I could eat a horse's ass.*"

Her smile quickly morphed into a small round "o" shape, and I smelled a quick pang of embarrassment. She was worried she'd just been too crude.

I laughed, and that put her immediately back at ease. I picked up another whiff of that heat she had for me, so I extended the laugh a little bit longer, just for the satisfaction of what that did to her. "What do you say we pop over to an Irish pub around the corner? There's no pasta on the menu, but they've got a steak and potato dish that'll knock your socks off."

"I'm game for some sock-knocking," she said, and hooked her right arm out for me to take it. "Lead on, Macduff."

*   *   *

"This rare edition of the short story *History of the Necronomicon*, so the legends go," Gail said, "was created using Anthropodermic bibliopegy."

"Anthropo-whatnow?" I asked.

I'd been listening to her explain numerous theories and legends surrounding H.P. Lovecraft's infamous *Necronomicon* and the mythology the author had created about a book that never existed. Except, of course, for the numerous true believers, occultists, pranksters, hoaxers, and conspiracy theorists, who continued to perpetuate the idea that the text, allegedly written in Arabic by Abdul Alhazred, was real.

Only, Gail explained, while there were libraries of numerous versions of the *Necronomicon*—not as many as there were interpretations of the King James Bible, but plenty enough—there was something the real collectors would kill for: the special and extremely rare edition of Lovecraft's seven-hundred-word short story, *History of the Necronomicon.*

"Anthropodermic bibliopegy," she said. "The practice of binding books in human skin."

"Ugh," I replied, disturbed by the topic, but I could not take my eyes off hers. She was an incredibly intense storyteller. I'd been hanging on her every word for the past three-quarters of an hour as she'd explained the background of Lovecraft's work and the particular fictional text and its history that I needed stories about.

I already had a dozen possibilities kicking around in the back of my head for where I could take this mystery I was writing. But Gail was still going strong and had shocked me with this latest revelation.

"It's an obviously rare form of bookbinding, particularly today, but it was done numerous times throughout history. And it dates back to the thirteenth century, with one of the earliest known examples being a French Bible."

"What, did people donate their skin for such projects? Or was it just done to them?"

"A combination of both. There is a book in the Surgeons' Hall Museum in Edinburgh bound in the flesh of a man by the name of Burke. He was found guilty of drugging and killing sixteen people to sell their bodies to an anatomist. He was executed, and his skin was used to bind a book with the following words embossed on the cover—'Burke's Skin Pocket Book. Executed 28 Jan 1829.'"

"Holy crap," I said. I thought I had written macabre things in my mystery novels, but that was something else. "That's one heck of a death sentence. Or death sentences I suppose."

I laughed nervously.

Gail didn't laugh. Her scent revealed that she hadn't even noticed my vain attempt at stupid humor. She was concentrating on the story she was sharing.

"Back to that *History of the Necronomicon* book: it was bound in human skin, but there's one more thing that makes it even more disturbing."

Gail paused to slowly lift her glass of Merlot to her lips and take a sip.

I didn't dare speak and break the storytelling spell she had me under. And I could tell from the scent she exuded that she knew she had me in the palm of her hand. She was enjoying the fact she had me on the edge of my seat.

"While they're not sure whose blood it is," she began to say as she carefully placed her now-empty wineglass back down, "blood was used as the ink for this particular, and very much sought-after, handwritten version of the book."

"Oh my God. That's perfect." I clapped my hands together to enunciate my point. "That can be the underlying book behind the murder, while everyone else thinks it's related to a different rare version of the *Necronomicon*."

I rubbed my clasped hands together and sat back for a moment, letting my eyes escape from hers to glance at the ceiling as I stored away a few nuggets of details for the novel.

"Yes," I muttered. "Yes, that can work really well."

I picked up my beer and took a sip of it. It was warm, having sat untouched for most of the past hour. But I didn't care. Gail's stories had helped fill me with the details I needed to break the block. I could feel the words itching to tumble out of me.

This was when I realized I wanted nothing more than to call for the check, pay the tab, and rush back to my room at the Algonquin, where I would write until the wee hours of the morning. Heck, I had enough here to carry me through to the very end of this book.

I loved it when it all fell into place.

"Huh," Gail said as I placed my beer back on the table. "So that's what it's like."

I turned my eyes and attention back to her. She was now leaning forward and staring at me, the look on her face and the scent coming off her indicating she was absolutely fascinated with what she'd just witnessed.

"That's what *what's* like?"

"That creative spark. Inspiration. Whatever it is, I could have sworn I saw the moment it flickered in your eyes. The air changed. You seemed to change. You went from a listener to being engaged in something a million miles away."

"Did I?"

"Yeah," she said, and her eyes sparkled with excitement. "It was such an amazing transformation to observe. You looked almost like you might be having an orgasm."

I laughed. "That's sometimes exactly how it feels."

"No kidding."

"Yeah."

"Where do your ideas come from?"

"Most of them come from a warehouse in Schenectady."

A confused look and feeling overcame her.

I laughed. "It's an old joke that science fiction writer Harlan Ellison once said in an interview. He was asked where his crazy ideas came from, and he said, *Schenectady*. There's a warehouse that ships him a pack of ideas for twenty-five bucks every week."

"Oh," she said, wrinkling her cute nose. I realized I'd shared an insider writer joke that made no sense to her.

"So," I said, "I got some amazing content that I can really use. But we haven't even ordered yet. And I'm even more famished than before."

Because Gail was so busy sharing details and I was so focused on listening, we hadn't looked at our menus. The waiter who had come by three times to try to take our order seemed to have given up on us ordering food.

We had, however, had a couple of rounds of drinks during that time. Or, at least, Gail had a couple of glasses of Merlot. I had my barely touched beer and a glass of water.

Our waiter noticed Gail's glass was empty and approached the table. We used that time to order some food. I went with the steak and potatoes while Gail ordered the famous Angry Burger.

"And," she said, "I think we should start with a pound of your crispy chicken wings. How hot do they come?"

"Buffalo or sweet and spicy."

She looked at me with a defiant look on her face. "Can you handle hot and spicy, Andrews?"

I wasn't a big fan of hot food. Frank's RedHot was typically more than enough for me. But I wasn't about to look like a wuss. "Sure," I said. "The hotter, the better."

"You've got nothing hotter than buffalo?" Gail asked the waiter.

"No. But I can put in a special request with the chef."

"You do that," she said. "Tell him he's dealing with a couple of spicy food pros. See if he can try to hurt us."

I may have physically winced at those words because I picked up on the waiter noticing my reaction.

"Are you sure? The chef can really spice them up."

"I'm sure." She looked at me again, challenging me to be the one to back down. "How about you?"

"One hundred percent," I lied.

"Oh," Gail said to the waiter," and forget the Merlot refill I just requested. I'll skip over to beer. Whatever it is that he's having."

Even though my own warm beer was three-quarters full, I told him I'd like another one. I figured I'd need the extra liquid to wash down the pain from the hot wings.

"Of course," the waiter said, departing to place our order.

That was rather gutsy of her. Ordering messy sauce wings on a first date. And a hot wings throwdown at that.

This isn't a date. This is a work meeting. And YOU need to get back home and work on this novel.

I shook my head as if that annoying voice was a fly buzzing around me.

"Are we going to have a hot wings challenge showdown or something?" I asked.

Gail grinned, and the magical twinkle in her eye set my heart on fire. I knew these wings would be too much for me, but she was already proving to be too much. The smile I was looking at could set a thousand hearts on fire. It was most certainly setting mine in flames.

"So, this series of books you write. These mysteries. What's the main character's name?"

"Maxwell Bronte."

"Bronte, like the literary sisters?"

"Yeah, exactly. I named him after Emily Brontë. Well, Bronte without those little umlauts over the E. I didn't want to constantly try to find the special characters on my keyboard, so I went with a regular E for my character."

"Why Emily Brontë?"

"*Wuthering Heights* was one of the first classic novels I loved reading when I was young."

"Wait a minute," she said. "You're a dude. That's a classic romance novel."

"It's a classic novel with themes of love, yes. But also theological conceptions of good and evil. It also explores revenge and obsession. It also challenged the Victorian morality of the time. And because it concerned itself with gender, it can be seen as an early feminist text."

"You are nothing like I'd expected you to be."

"You as well."

"So let's get back to Maxwell Bronte. His name came from Emily Brontë. But where did the character come from? Where did his personality come from? I'm curious to hear how you created this guy."

It was my turn to ramp up the storyteller mode as Gail listened to me share the backstory of the character whose novels were responsible for my fame and fortune.

I paused when the wings arrived at the table.

"The chef was able to make something extra hot, extra spicy. He calls these wings his *Afterburn Delight Special*."

I had been able to smell the intensity of whatever hot sauce the chef had come up with well before the wings reached the table, and I was sweating at the very scent of them.

Feeling a sneeze coming on, inspired by the spices tingling my nose, I turned my head and let out three sharp, sneezy bursts.

This wasn't going to be good.

"Okay," Gail said, taking a quick drink of her beer. "The game is this: whoever can eat the most wings without first taking a drink wins."

She easily kicked my ass.

I was only halfway through chewing my first bite when the overpowering heat of the sauce, intensified by my overly hyper taste buds, forced me to take a sip of my beer.

Gail had already polished off her second wing by the time I picked that first wing back up.

"Really?" she said around a mouthful of food. "One bite in?"

Damn, she was even cute when she spoke with food in her mouth. I looked at the smear of hot sauce on her left cheek and wanted to reach out and remove it with the tip of my finger.

But I would never make such a bold move like that.

"Okay," I said, "I'll admit it. I'm not into hot food. But you're going at it like a champion."

She dropped the third de-meated bone into the little basket beside the wing plate and picked up a fourth one. "I'm on a roll," she said. "Going to see how many of these babies I can polish off before I have to take a drink. You'd better eat up. Or they'll be gone before you finish the first one." She snorted a laugh.

Again, the snort—like seeing her talk with food in her mouth—was endearing. I loved that she didn't give a shit and bypassed putting on airs of being ladylike. She was authentically herself, and I relished seeing that.

There were two separate mini bowls of the blue cheese sauce. I dipped my wing into it, completely smothering it, then took another bite. That made it almost bearable. I drank down most of my beer before finishing the first wing.

I drowned the second wing in the blue cheese sauce and took alternating bites of the celery sticks on our plate between wing bites.

The experience was painful, but I was extremely hungry and looked forward to the sustenance.

I soaked the third wing in my glass of water, diluting much of the hot sauce before taking a bite.

"Hey!" Gail said, her lips now smothered in the hot sauce. I wondered what it would be like to kiss those lips—after they were wiped clean of the hot sauce, of course. "That's cheating!"

"I already lost a long time ago."

As I watched her continue to work her way through the wings, not once stopping to take a drink, I marveled at this unique woman. She was pushing forth despite the pain I could sense she was feeling, despite the sweat glistening on her forehead and the fact her nose was running.

I knew I should call it a night and get back to my hotel room now that I had what I needed to get past that writer's block.

But I couldn't resist spending more time with this woman. Even if it was only to see what she did, what she said next.

The main entrées came just as she was finishing off the full plate, and I was finishing my third wing.

"I have an idea for this round," I said. "No contests. How about we just eat like civilized adults."

"Hardee har," she said and took a drink of her beer.

We both started into the meals in front of us, and it was quiet for about a minute before Gail put her fork down and grinned mischievously at me.

"For the main entrée, we'll recognize the peace treaty. But when the desserts come around, the war is back on, my friend."

I laughed, wondering what sort of challenge or throwdown she might have planned for that. But more than that, I was happy to know she was planning on staying for a third course.

This was a night I simply did not want to end.

And technically, it didn't. Throughout the meal, she continued to inquire about my writing background. When it was time for dessert, the game she wanted to play was us guessing the other one's favorite dessert and ordering it.

We tied that round. But it was relatively easy. There were only three items on their menu. Apple tartlet, chocolate salted caramel soufflé, and mini pumpkin cheesecake.

I got her on the soufflé, and she pegged me on the cheesecake.

Long after the desserts were done, we kept asking for refills on our coffees. Gail told me the story of acquiring the occult shop and managing it with her friend Isabeau.

We kept talking, bouncing back and forth between sharing various stories of our lives, and it felt like the entire several hours of that meal took no more than about fifteen minutes.

Time can be like that when you click with a person. And I felt myself really clicking with Gail.

We closed that restaurant down, and the conversation, sharing, joking, and laughing continued between us until they started turning the lights out and putting chairs up on the tables. We finally got the not so subtle hints it was time to leave.

But instead of saying good night and parting ways, we walked together toward Times Square and the theater district, and then back and forth along the streets, as if we were exploring the area and targeting hitting them all, like trick-or-treaters trying to maximize our reach across the neighborhood.

The next thing I knew, we were still walking and engaged in animated conversation, and the sun was rising in the eastern sky.

We had been talking all. Damn. Night.

That had never happened to me before.

By the time we said goodbye, I knew only one thing.

This was a woman I wanted to—no, that I *needed* to see again.

Monday, May 23, 2011

Chapter Six

GAIL

"There's the woman I want to see," Isabeau called out when she walked into the store. Her thick black locs were woven into an elaborate knot on the crown of her head, an arrangement that would have weakened the muscles of mere mortals. But, as usual, Iz strode in with a ramrod straight back, her long neck sturdy and upright.

"Am I in trouble again?" I asked, though I already knew the answer. I had replied to her texts throughout the night, assuring her that I was okay, just talking, everything was fine. But I'd known while I walked the city with Michael that there would be hell to pay today.

"Let's go through your last few lovers, shall we? I want you to remind me who you are attracted to."

I groaned, and Isabeau held up her hand, her delicate fingers topped with black-painted talons spread out so she could enumerate her undoubtedly correct and copious points.

"Peter," she said, putting her thumb into her palm.

"Oh, that's not fair," I said. "That was years ago. Decades."

"It was four years ago. What was wrong with him?"

"He cheated. And had B.O."

She snapped didn't laugh at my joke, which is how I knew I was in trouble. "What about that Norwegian dude? Nils Nilson?"

"You know damn well that wasn't his name."

"Tell me, then." She still had her four fingers up in the air, and she was actually licking her lips with anticipation.

"Lars," I said, just wanting to get the conversation over with.

"Oh, that's right. Lars Lorenson, the Norwegian tattoo artist who forgot to tell his wife they were in a poly relationship. Therefore, also a cheater. Who came after that? Let's see…Mick. Bloody Mick. The aging rock star who lived in a Fifth Avenue penthouse and drank bathtub gin. And then there was Nessie, who I thought was nice enough."

"Except every time I went looking for her, she disappeared."

"Of course. She disappeared. To cheat. And after her came Jonathan?"

"Thomas."

"Ah, yes. Thomas. What was his deal?"

"He liked young women on the internet."

She smacked her forehead melodramatically. "Of course! It wasn't *technically* cheating because it was all virtual! Then came Jonathan, who bled you dry emotionally and financially. And cheated."

I sighed, and she opened her hand again. I'm not sure if she was about to reiterate a point or show off those nails. Honestly, I knew what she spent every week at the salon, and if I was her, I would enumerate everything too.

"In summary," she said, "we had a Yeti, an ogre, a Kraken, the Loch Ness monster, a Tommyknocker, and an emotional vampire. Did I miss anyone?"

I shook my head. She was not technically wrong about any of it.

"So, your new guy," she said.

"He's not my new guy!" I said very loudly, but my point was diminished because a group of goth teens entered the store. "Hello, Goddesses!" I saw how the girls were instantly entranced by Isabeau's gravelly voice and the glitter she dusted across her high cheekbones.

Iz wafted her very expensive hand through the air, practically hypnotizing them. "As you can see, we are having some construction problems," she said. "All that merchandise up front is half off. It has honey damage but is still spiritually functional. There are hand wipes on the counter if you get sticky."

When not overrun by feral bees, our store is actually a very well-appointed, classy place. Iz and I had painted the rich green walls ourselves, and installed dark wood flooring, where we placed baskets full of handwoven blankets, sage bundles, and incense packets.

The girls rushed to the clearance table, and Iz turned back to me.

"Now that we've established why you should not be allowed to date, let's reiterate the vow of celibacy that you swore."

I hated it so, so much when she was right.

"Can we just get to work?" I asked. "I've gotten three more estimates from pest control companies, and the only one that was a lower price than yesterday's guy was the one who showed up this morning with no shirt on. He wanted me to see the gigantic bee tattoo on his belly."

"Cool," Iz replied. "Why didn't you hire anyone?"

"Two reasons. For one, we have to find a bee-friendly company. Meaning, we can't let them kill the bees."

"Obviously," Iz agreed.

"Second, the bee-friendly companies tend to be about five times more expensive. Len, of course, is not willing to pay. He says bees are pests, and he'll just take a hose up there and clean it out himself."

Isabeau snorted. "I'd love to see that."

The door opened again and another woman walked inside.

When I mention that I run an occult shop, everyone assumes it's full of stoners, hippies, and black-leather-clad Satan worshipers. We do have a few of those types, but most people would be surprised by the diversity of our clientele. We have a lot of devoted occult practitioners, but many of our clients are just curious shoppers or history buffs. Some are disillusioned with modern religion, some want to try a magic spell. A lot of people want costumes or props, which we don't carry, but they usually leave with a nice scented candle for their suburban home. The people who want the darker magic supplies know what to look for, and I've learned not to judge anyone who walks in. This new customer was as straight-edge as a woman could be, dressed in a chic camel-colored pantsuit, with shiny hair cut into a sharp pixie.

Iz repeated her sales spiel to the woman and turned back to me. I kept my eyes on the customer, who seemed tense and skittish, her eyes continually darting over at me.

"So, my suggestion is we liquidate now and start looking for a new location," I murmured to Iz, whose eyes widened.

"You want to quit?"

"I said find a new location," I said firmly. "Not quit. By the time this bee issue is resolved, we may have lost too much business to recover. Why not get out while we can?"

"We have an annual lease."

"Breaking it might be cheaper than shoveling money into the shop to keep it afloat while Len the Lizard sorts out his life."

The woman looked up at me again, and when she realized I was staring right at her, she attempted a weak smile. *Just try me, bitch,* I thought. I can usually spot a klepto a mile away. This one didn't fit the usual profile, but if she thought she would walk out of here with a tarot deck stuffed in her no-doubt-very-expensive French bra, she was going to find out what happens when you piss off a brunette.

When my phone rang, I glanced down at the screen and tried to hide the shiver of pleasure that ran through me when I saw Michael Andrews' phone number. I felt the woman watching me more openly now, so I murmured, "Lydia's here," to Iz and answered the phone.

As soon as I said it, Iz snapped to attention and her sharp eyes locked on the woman. You don't ever want to tip off a potential thief that you are on to them in case they turn out not to be a thief. People tend to get angry at the accusation. Iz and I had come up with the code word while watching *Beetlejuice* on television because Winona Ryder played Lydia. All I can say is, it made perfect sense when we were stoned.

The back wall of our store used to hold several beautiful altars, but it was now bare, except for the streaks of honey running down the green paint. I leaned in close to it and breathed in the spicy-sweet scent. Cloves and marshmallows. My mouth watered. I was suddenly hyperaware of how my hips moved as I spoke to him. Swaying languidly left and right, like I was keeping time with a song in my head. Did I actually *giggle*? I noticed my finger drifting along the curve of the shelf, and it stopped in a pool of honey that had gathered in the corner. I put my finger in my mouth and the sugar melted onto my tongue. My senses overloaded with the heady sweetness of warm honey and the low murmur of Michael's deep, growling voice.

When the call ended, I took a breath and turned back to the store. I could feel a hot flush on my face, but overall thought I had held it together pretty well. The woman was still there, but the teens had left.

Iz narrowed her dark eyes at me. "You're meeting him tonight."

"Yes. To work with him. For money. Which we need, in case you hadn't noticed."

"Where are you going?" This question came from the woman. She didn't have any merchandise in her hand, but she was leaning up against the counter, arms splayed out as if she was telling us a secret.

"For dinner?" I asked. "I don't know. Some Thai place."

"What time?"

I glanced at Isabeau. "Um. Why?"

"Oh." She laughed and looked fake-embarrassed, as if I'd just caught her in a really meaningless lie. "No reason. I am just looking forward to trying something new tonight. I don't really know much about Thai food, so if I see you there, maybe you can help me with the menu."

Yeah, right. Twenty-five thousand restaurants in New York City, and you want to go to the one I'm going to? I don't think so, lady.

This one was creeping me out, and that was saying a lot from an occult shop owner. I leveled her with my coolest gaze and was glad I had worn my black lipstick today. Sometimes it's nice to have a face like mine— resting bitch face, the kids call it, which is totally unfair. Still, when I'm really mad, I can go dark in one second flat, and it does come in handy. "I'm sure the waiters can help you read a menu. Is there anything else you need from us?"

The woman left without another word.

"Well, that was bizarre," Iz commented.

I didn't answer. Something about this encounter had unsettled me.

"Maybe she was trying to ask you out?"

"You wish," I retorted.

"As a matter of fact, I do wish," Iz replied. "Because if you go out with her, you can't go out with the writer. Andrew what's-his-name."

"Michael Andrews. I know you know who he is—we watched that Maxwell Bronte miniseries together."

She didn't reply.

"How about this," I said. "I amend my previous vow. Celibacy means I won't have sex. But I can date if a nice person comes along. Isn't that healthy? Wouldn't you like that for me? Maybe that's a super mature way to find a good partner. I can have leisurely dates and get to know people intimately for a long time. After a year, if any of them pass my—and your—entrance exam, I will invite them into my boudoir." I overpronounced the word *boooo-dwaaa*, because it always makes Iz laugh when I pretend to speak French.

"Just know this," she said. "I will pick you up every time you fall, Gail Sommers. Every single time. You know I will. But I want you to know that I have less energy for it each time you repeat the same mistake."

My eyes unexpectedly filled with tears, and I pulled her into a hug. No one in the history of best friends has ever had a best friend better than me.

But she and I don't necessarily tell each other everything.

For example, she didn't know that at this very moment, there was a brand-new pack of condoms in my purse.

Chapter Seven

MICHAEL
1:48 p.m.

"Should I go out and pick up a pack of condoms before I meet with her tonight?" I asked.

Asking that made me feel like I was seventeen again and about to go on my first date.

Not only did Buddy give off an air of extreme discomfort, but he had a look on his face like I'd just offered him rotten meat for dinner.

I realized two things immediately.

One was that after almost a decade of living here, I didn't have any real friends in this city. I knew and regularly interacted with plenty of folks on a continual basis, but they were all people I had a working relationship with. The ones I connected with the most were Mack, my fantastic agent, and his assistant Anne.

And while Mack's work helped propel my career forward, I would never mistake the gruff, crude, and aggressive man for a friend. Sure, he was responsible for getting me into seven-figure annual earnings as a writer, but I had no doubt that if I stopped producing, he'd drop me faster than a politician drops his promises.

Anne was one of the sweetest and kindest people I'd ever met, and we got along like gangbusters, but it wasn't as if we were besties.

I got along quite well with most of the staff at the Algonquin Hotel, which I'd been calling home for a little over a year now. Paul—one of the doormen—and I had regular conversations. But we only ever spoke standing in the front entranceway or just outside the hotel.

Frighteningly, I realized that my closest friend in New York City, Buddy, a traveling salesman, didn't even live in the Big Apple. I saw him perhaps a half dozen times a year when he had business in the city.

The second thing was despite the fact Buddy was the single person I'd spent the most time in one-on-one conversations with for much of the last decade, I had never once shared anything truly intimate or related to my love life with him.

Well, that part was easy. I didn't really have a love life. I had a work life. And a writing life. And just a few years ago, my work life and writing life became the same thing.

The only truly unique thing I did other than eat, write, and sleep, was that I morphed into a gray wolf and romped around after sundown on all fours for about ten days every month.

At least it got me out of the house.

But that thing that provided some variety in my life was also the thing preventing me from having any serious relationships. Nobody knew about my affliction, nor the special strength and sensory abilities I retained when in my normal human form.

So it would be extremely awkward trying to keep a long-term relationship when you had to pretty much disappear every night for a week and a half.

Oh, don't mind me, honey. I will be out all night howling at the moon, sniffing other wolves' butts, and maybe stalking and devouring a few rabbits and other small rodents. But I'll be back early enough to have the coffee on for you before you wake up.

Yeah, I didn't think so.

I realized Buddy was still sitting there wordlessly, his bulbous nose still wrinkled in confusion and perhaps disgust, his eyebrows raised, and his eyes wide, making him look even more like Buddy Hackett.

This might have been the longest I'd ever seen him at a lack for words.

"This is a working relationship, right?" he finally asked.

"Yeah,"

"So why would you need condoms?"

"Well…" I couldn't tell him I knew she had the hots for me because I smelled it off her, so I went with the other potentially obvious reason. "After dinner last night, we walked and talked all night. The entire night. The conversation was stimulating and nonstop. We didn't even notice the time passing and that the sun was coming up."

"When you and I met, we regularly had nonstop conversations that lasted all night. That didn't mean we wanted to jump in bed with one another."

I made an effort to keep a wry grin from sprouting on my face. Most of my conversations with Buddy were extremely one-sided affairs. Particularly the longer ones. They were less of the back-and-forth variety of most verbal intercourse and more like a one-man show performing a monologue to a one-man audience. "This is different. She's—"

"She's sexy. I get it. But she's also a work contact. You can't confuse the intimacy of the interview and research this conversation was about with personal intimacy."

"But we talked about more than details for my novel. We talked about ourselves. We shared things about our lives."

"That was just a thing that salespeople do to make their customers feel more relaxed and comfortable. I do it all the time.

"People buy things from others they know, like, and trust. So the key to being a great salesperson—and trust me, this is my entire livelihood—is charming them. We're all at least a bit narcissistic. The most absolutely captivating thing often revolves around ourselves and our own lives.

"When I meet a potential sales target, do you know what I do? I look into their background. Are they married? Do they have kids or pets? Where did they grow up? What sports team do they root for? I make sure to sprinkle plenty of questions about these things into my conversation to put them at ease, to relax them. People love thinking about and talking about themselves. I'm offering them an instant conduit to feeling good about who they are, what they do, all that they have accomplished. It's ego stroking.

"As a salesperson, I'm constantly playing people, always looking for a way I can gain some livelihood out of the relationship.

"Remember, she is a salesperson who owns and runs a small business. I don't need to meet her to know that she's got to be adept at schmoozing and making her customers feel comfortable, appreciated, and listened to."

"But she's not selling anything to me."

"Isn't she? You don't know what her ulterior motive is. This could be a play for a longer-term con. She's providing you information and helping you out. Just be prepared for the other shoe to drop on this. You never know. This could be a reciprocity thing. You've always been naïve, always wanted to see the good in people. But this world is full of people with hidden agendas. And who's to say she doesn't have one?"

When he said that, I considered how I might have also been using Gail.

And not just as a source for information and in-depth research about the occult. She was also an inspiration for writing.

Because I hadn't slept when I got back home.

Instead, I went right to my laptop and hammered out six thousand words in the book I had been previously blocked on. It had been weeks since I'd written more than a few hundred.

The writing I was doing didn't even involve the *Necronomicon*. But Gail had kick-started those creative juices in me like nothing ever had before.

And I realized I'd been writing nonstop until the time I got the call from Buddy, asking if I was free to meet at a diner just down the street from the Algonquin for lunch. This was one of his quick in-and-out trips through town.

I was running on a combination of adrenaline, at least a half dozen cups of coffee, and the high of having spent the night engaged in the most dynamic conversation with a captivating and beautiful woman.

"This wasn't a work thing," I said.

"I'll bet it's a work thing for her. Understanding your agent like I do, I bet Mack slipped her a few bucks to meet with you."

"Bullshit!"

Buddy shook his head, picked up the white ceramic coffee mug, and held it in front of his mouth for a quick moment, staring at me quietly. His eyes took on a gravity I'd never seen him relay before. "Listen, son, I know you're infatuated with this woman. I know she seems to have you under some sort of mystical spell. I can see it in your eyes.

"But please just do me a favor and take this thing slow. If there's something there, there's no need to rush into anything.

"And maybe be careful what you share with her. Don't put too much trust in her, or too much stock in what's being delivered on the surface.

"This woman sells things for a living. You might be best advised to play your cards close to your chest. She'll likely be able to see things about you that you don't want to be known.

"Everybody has a past, some sort of things best left in the dark. Try not to share too much about yourself in these conversations."

I thought about what Buddy said.

And, as he sometimes did, it felt like he was trying to tell me something without telling me something. He sometimes spoke in riddles. Confusing riddles, but often with a hidden message.

He didn't know about my werewolf curse. But over the years he occasionally referenced things that made me wonder if he really knew the truth and was keeping it such a tightly guarded secret that he wouldn't even put that out in the air between us.

And he couldn't know I'd been thinking about revealing my secret to Gail. Who else in this city would actually believe me if not an expert on the occult? Also, sharing this curse with someone who could understand and perhaps help me understand what I was also appealed to me.

He glanced at his watch and put his coffee back down. "Oh jeez, I've got to go. I need to be about twenty blocks from here, then I need to hit the highway for Philadelphia for a morning meeting there tomorrow."

"Go," I said to him, perhaps more briskly than I intended. I was angry at him for suggesting that Gail, a sharp, hot woman I was infatuated with, had an ulterior motive. "I'll pick up the check."

"Thanks. I'm supposed to be back in the Big Apple before the end of June. This time for a longer stay. Maybe we can catch a Yankees game. I know a guy who can get us good seats."

Buddy knew I didn't like sports but that I did enjoy going to Yankee Stadium and soaking in the ambiance of the experience. It was always good for my writing. I also recognized this was his way of subtly apologizing to me for being such a downer about Gail.

"Catch you later, Wolfman Jack," he said as he headed toward the exit. "And a word to the wise: slow your roll."

I was reminded of the various wolf nicknames he'd used for me over the years. It was his cheeky nod to the way we'd met on that lonely highway in upstate New York all those years ago. His car had shown up at just the right time to save me from a wolf attack. So Buddy thought it was funny to call me Wolfman or some variation on it.

As I watched him stroll down the street, his portly body shuffling a lot faster than a man of his size should be able to comfortably move, I thought a bit about what he said.

And about the call I'd made to Gail on my walk over to have lunch with Buddy. I'd told her I had a few more questions I'd like to ask about the *Necronomicon* and, remembering her love of hot and spicy food, I suggested a great Thai place I'd been to several times.

From the sound of her voice, she'd been really into it.

It had been that feeling making me wonder if I should prepare by getting a pack of condoms.

While there were more things I could ask her about the occult and that Lovecraft text, it would be intriguing to find out what she knew about werewolves.

Using her to see if I could figure out more about my condition was as appealing as wanting to know what her lips tasted like, what it would feel like to hold her tight in my arms.

But I also reflected on Buddy's words of concern. There was something in him referring to me as Wolfman and cautioning me to not reveal too much that created a disturbing sour pang in my gut and unsettled me.

*   *   *

7:14 p.m.

Though I was pretty sure I was walking with an excited spring in my step, I had to keep reminding myself that I should proceed with extreme care tonight.

I was still about a block away from the Thai restaurant just south of the Flatiron District, where I'd made a seven thirty reservation. It was basically a half hour walk straight down either Sixth or Fifth Avenues from my place.

Only I realized less than fifteen minutes had passed, and I was nearly there. I'd been walking really fast.

Of course I was. I couldn't wait to see Gail again, to fall helplessly into those gorgeous green eyes. To imagine what it might be like to be staring into them from an inch away while our lips touched.

I shuddered in delight at the thought.

Slow your roll.

Buddy's words came back to me and I almost stopped in my tracks.

What the hell had I been thinking earlier? I couldn't tell Gail about my werewolf nature. We'd just met.

Sure, we'd talked for hours and traded stories back and forth, but we didn't know one another. How much could we learn about one another in that short time span?

I told myself I should play it cool.

I wouldn't tell her.

In fact, given her keen sense of observation, I should do everything I could not to tip my hand at the extraordinary powers I have. With Gail's background and her insights into the occult and the paranormal, she, more than anyone else, would likely be able to somehow be on to me, and on to my true nature.

Curbing my enthusiasm would help.

Maybe it would help to distance myself a bit. Play it chill. And all the while, try to ignore my natural instinct to rely on my enhanced wolf senses. I didn't drink much, and sometimes alcohol can help slightly mute my senses. So maybe I'd make an effort to get more alcohol in me as early as possible.

Muting my sense of smell and hearing would help me be less intuitive. Be less able to read her intense desire for me. Because that, in and of itself, was a huge turn-on.

Landing on that conclusion, I started walking again. This time with a fixed and forceful determination. I wasn't a schoolboy hoping to go on a date and get kissed by a cute girl. I was a professional man on a mission to get the information I needed for my book.

"Just the facts, ma'am," I muttered as I walked, trying to conjure up the cold and emotionless tone of Joe Friday from that old television show.

The *Dragnet* tune played in my head as I continued my purposeful march down Broadway.

But the music in my head stopped when I spotted her walking half a block ahead. She bisected Broadway in her walk west along East Nineteenth Street. The restaurant we were meeting at was about halfway down that block.

When I got to the corner, I was able to pick up her scent and paused for a moment to bask in it.

Oh yes, I was so damn into this woman that just the scent of her set my heart racing.

Cool it. Slow your roll. Chillax.

I wasn't sure if that was my voice or Buddy's. All I knew was that neither one of us had ever used the term "chillax" before.

Gail's voice drifted to me from up the street.

"Here you go," she was saying. I saw her bending over and speaking to an elderly woman sitting on the sidewalk, leaning against the brick wall. The woman and her clothes smelled of weeks-old sweat that carried all this way, and her face was lined and worn from a combination of age and stress. I know I tagged her as elderly, but she might have actually been no more than mid-forties based on the beat of her heart.

"Thank you, sweetheart," the woman said. Her voice was dry and gravelly.

"What's your name, love?" Gail said.

"Mary."

"Nice to meet you, Mary. My name is Gail. This twenty-dollar bill is all I have on me. I don't carry much cash. But I can order you something from inside and bring it out. I also own a store on Avenue B near Tompkins Square Park. It's called Enchanting Magic. We open at nine o'clock. If you come by tomorrow, I'll have more for you, and some fresh clothes. We only have a few T-shirts, but I'm sure we'll have something in your size."

"God bless you, ma'am," Mary said, choking on the tears of appreciation.

"Please call me Gail."

"God bless you, Gail."

I stopped walking, not wanting to get too close so that Gail saw me as they discussed what food Gail might be able to order and bring out for her.

When it was decided, and Mary thanked her again, Gail got down on one knee, leaned in, and hugged Mary.

Then she got up, said she'd see her soon, and walked up the street and into the entrance of the restaurant.

I shook my head.

How the heck was I going to be able to play it cool for someone so incredibly compassionate and thoughtful like that?

Tuesday, May 24, 2011

Chapter Eight

GAIL

I didn't know how the hell I was supposed to play it cool around thousands of swarming bees, but one thing I did know was that being stuck in a closet-sized attic space with a clumsy doofus who had an ego the size of Texas did not make my heart rate slow down. Not to mention his bright yellow shirt with the *Plan Bee!* logo in a jagged black font was getting on my last nerve.

I stifled a yawn. Staying up two nights in a row, talking to Michael and wishing he would kiss me, was also not helping my patience.

"All bees are male, you see, and they want to serve the queen. There is only one queen. Her only job is to bear their children. So if we kill the queen, your problem is solved. No more babies."

Seriously? Even I knew more than this clown, and I'd been learning about bees for all of two days.

He'd been saying shit like this since he arrived for our consultation an hour ago, and I was ready to kick him out within the first five minutes. But he was also the first out of all of the pest control people who invited me into the attic with him, and I wasn't going to pass up that opportunity. So I stood there, holding my body still, calming my breath, while a sentient turnip incorrectly explained false facts about bee culture to me. The air in the attic was hot, and the low thrumming sound from the bees caused us to speak louder than normal. Every time he spoke, they seemed to get even louder, as if attempting to drown out his words.

"Do you keep hives?"

"You can't keep beehives in the city."

I clenched my teeth. Was I really going to have to bee-splain to this supposed professional? A bee landed on my blouse, and I stared down at her, watching her make her way over the hills and valleys of my chest. I didn't want to startle her, so I spoke slowly.

"Actually, you can," I said. "It was legalized in 2010. People keep beehives all over the city. Do you ever get stung?"

"Hundreds of times. Every single day," he answered. "It comes with the job."

Not for people who know what they're doing.

"Tell me what you will do with the bees once you remove them," I asked.

He turned back to the gigantic hive and stuck the handle of his axe into the waxy yellow cells. I could see the bees becoming agitated—were bees capable of agitation? Did they have emotions? All I could see was that they seemed to be flying around rather lazily before, but every time he jabbed the hive, they got a little hyper. I can't say I blamed them.

"I'll dump 'em," he said. "Far from you."

"But you won't kill them."

"Oh, the extraction process kills them. It's like a giant vacuum."

"But," I began, and then I lowered my voice again. The bee on my shirt had been joined by a friend. "Everyone knows you're not supposed to kill bees."

We were interrupted by a gentle tapping on the door that led to the back stairs. Plan Bee and I looked at each other in alarm, and then I turned very slowly to open the door, my finger already up at my lips. It was probably Isabeau coming to check on me and this Disney villain of a beekeeper.

Michael's eyes traveled down my shirt, but instead of checking me out (which, I'm not going to lie, I wouldn't have minded), I suspect he was alarmed at the bees crawling on me.

I turned back.

"Thanks for your time," I said, to Plan Bee. "My next appointment is here. I'll be in touch after I get a few more estimates."

Michael took one step into the attic space and froze, noticing the wildlife lesson happening around me and the sweaty fellow who was still expounding on the dangers of killer bees. The bees, their home invaded by three rather large humans, were moving faster now, darting around us and buzzing loudly.

Plan Bee gathered his supplies and hooked his axe into a loop on his belt buckle. So help me, pagan gods above, he had an axe on his belt. Perhaps understanding the situation, Michael looked me straight in the eye and said, in a totally deadpan voice, "Benson Honeywell from Bee Our Guest Bee Control. Bee-witched to meet you."

"Enchantée," I drawled in my most syrupy voice. "My name is Bee-yonce Bee-gonia."

He tried not to smile, but I saw the hint of that smirk. I held out my hand and he shook it. An electric current ran through our palms so quickly that I thought I'd been stung by one of the errant bees. It was only the second time we'd touched. When we'd parted at dawn this morning, he'd leaned in for one of those friendly kisses you give someone you're not really close to. His lips didn't even touch me, only the stubbly part of his cheek rested on mine for a second, but I'd swear that spot had been on fire ever since. Having sex with this guy would probably electrocute me. Not that I was going to have sex with him, obviously. I was on a celibate year, no matter how many condoms I stuffed into my purse.

"What seems to *bee* the problem, little lady?" he asked.

Fortunately, the door closed behind Plan Bee, so we could both relax our shoulders and laugh. Not too loudly, of course. We were still surrounded by two hundred thousand bees.

Michael stood with his back against the wall and took in the scene. The water heater, pipes, and furnace took up most of the room. The bees had built a massive hive over the electrical wiring on the opposite wall, and it was a truly spectacular sight. As we had suspected, rodents had gotten into the hive, and giant chunks lay on the floor. Honey still dripped from the gaping wounds. The remaining combs lay atop each other like a stack of golden plates, and the entire mass was pulsing with the movement of thousands of bees swarming over it. Hundreds more flew in lazy circles around the room, sometimes darting in and out of the vent in the ceiling. The air in the room had a heavy texture, heady with the spicy-sweet scent of honey and the thick drone of their buzzing. Michael seemed to sense that he was the intruder, and his body had gone still while he watched.

"Are you scared?" he asked me.

"Not anymore," I said. "I was while that fool was swinging his axe around. It's amazing they didn't sting him to death."

"I don't know much about bees," he murmured. We were almost whispering, as if this was holy ground. I hadn't moved from when we shook hands, and we were so close that I could hear him take a deep breath. "Do you?"

"Just what I've learned in the last few days," I said. "They really are harmless unless you threaten them."

"Most animals are," Michael breathed.

A bee came close to my ear, and I felt it tangle in my hair. My instinct was to flail around wildly, but I remained still. Michael, without panic, lifted the chunk of hair off my shoulder and the bee flew away. He let the hair slide out of his fingers and drift down onto my shoulder slowly, almost strand by strand, without taking his eyes from mine.

"How did you know where to find me?" I whispered.

"I went into the shop. Isabeau told me you were up here."

Uh-oh.

"What did she—I mean, what did you think of her?" I asked.

"Nice," he murmured. "Until she told me that she'd cut my balls off with a rusty spoon if I hurt you."

Oh, lord.

"Why would she think I'm going to hurt you?"

"It's nothing, really. I'm supposed to be celibate for a year. I've had a string of rather bad relationships, and she's very protective."

"But this isn't a relationship," he said. His voice had gone even lower, and he was so close to my ear that the skin on my neck goosefleshed. His fingers drifted off my hair, and he traced a line down my shoulder and slowly down my arm to my wrist, where a bee was resting. His finger stopped there, but he didn't move away from me.

"No, I know it's not a relationship," I stammered. "It can't be anything. I made a vow."

"Are you a nun?"

I laughed, but very quietly. The humming had settled into a low, hypnotic rhythm, and I had the strangest sensation that Michael and I were swaying on our feet. Almost waltzing. I thought about what it must feel like to slow dance with him, rest my cheek against the soft linen of his shirt, and let his strong arms move me around a room. The picture in my head made me feel drunk.

"Hardly," I said. "I'm just trying to protect my heart from rodent invaders."

"By all means," he said. "Hearts are fragile. That's why this is a purely professional relationship."

We were standing so close that when I nodded, the tip of my nose bumped onto his shoulder. He really was impossibly tall.

"All business," I agreed.

His eyes traveled over my hair, my face, my shirt. The bees darted between us as if we were part of their ecosystem.

"If we stay here long enough, do you think they'll cover us with honeycombs?" he asked.

"Maybe," I said. "But we'd never be able to move without destroying their home."

"Hmm. So the last thing I would see would be...you. Your eyes."

My chest ached as I took a trembling breath. I desperately wanted to kiss him, to sting his lips with my teeth. Bees walked all over his shirt, but he didn't flinch.

"Tell me something else you know about bees," he whispered in my ear.

I took a deep breath, the scent of honey so ripe it dizzied me. "Males die after mating," I said. "Which seems awfully unfair to them, if you ask me."

He shrugged. "I suppose it depends on who they mated with. Maybe they are perfectly happy to die for that one woman."

"Maybe. But wouldn't you give it up? If you knew it would destroy your life, wouldn't you just avoid sex forever? Who needs that kind of agony?"

"Maybe they think it's ecstasy. Maybe in the bee world, making love to the queen is the highest level of nirvana. Maybe they dream about it, and they die knowing they've done one truly great thing with their life."

"Listen, I'm not saying I don't want a few of the men I've been with to die, exactly," I said, moving an inch closer to him. I couldn't see his face clearly anymore, and instead focused on his neck. He was freshly shaven, and I had a sudden, absolutely insane urge to run my tongue over his Adam's apple. I remembered his suggestion about eating honey off the dripping wall, and I shivered. "I'm just saying I've never once met someone I'm willing to die for. I'd rather stay celibate."

"I've never once regretted falling for someone, even if they hurt me in the end," he said. "It's worth it. I want someone to love me so much she will rip me open with her fangs."

"Jesus!" I said, startled into a laugh. "Are we still talking about sex? That sounds extreme."

He looked a little embarrassed, and I wanted to pull him into me and tell him he could rip me open with his fangs any day of the week. But we remained still and quiet, locked in the erotic, honeyed heaviness of the room.

"All I meant was that when I finally open myself up to someone, I give in fully. I don't want to hold back."

"Why?"

He turned his head toward me, inhaled deeply, and closed his eyes. "That's not a life."

"No," I breathed. "It isn't."

His lips parted, and he moved forward a fraction of an inch. Just a bee sting closer, and I could have tasted him.

But he stopped and said, "I was wondering if you want to have a drink with me tonight."

"Is this a professional drink?" I asked.

"Strictly business," he replied. "I have all sorts of questions for you about…" His voice drifted off, and I lifted my head to look him in the eyes, which were vaguely unfocused. "About work," he finished.

"Where?"

"Why don't we meet in the lobby of the Algonquin?"

"Mmmmm," I sighed. "That's my favorite hotel in the city."

His mouth moved into an agonizingly slow smile. "I'll see you there," he said. "Are you going to walk out with me?"

"No," I said. "I want to watch the bees for a few more minutes."

"You should hire a female beekeeper," he said. "I don't think they'd hurt the bees."

He used his hands to gently brush the bees off his shirt and opened the door. He glanced at me once before he shut it, and his eyebrow went up. "Don't *bee* late."

I groaned, but couldn't help laughing.

Why was he willing to give in fully, without counting the cost? And what good was protecting my heart from a man like him? A callused heart might not ache anymore, but did it beat properly?

I pulled out my phone and texted Isabeau, who had no doubt seen Michael leave and had some choice words for me.

Maybe celibacy can mean not moving in with anyone for a full year.

I clicked my ringer off, put the phone back in my pocket, and watched the bees settle again.

My vow of celibacy wasn't written in blood, after all. I was fairly certain it wasn't legally binding.

Chapter Nine

MICHAEL
8:15 p.m.

Every time I thought about Gail, I had to keep reminding myself about that book bound in human flesh and written in blood.

She had, after all, told me about it. And that disturbing image helped me focus on the macabre and not the warm way Gail made me feel when she smiled at me, or, like earlier today when we had been standing so close together.

So.

Close.

Together.

Picturing that dark and eerie book steered me back to the real reason I wanted to meet with her, and why I needed to keep seeing her. She was a source for my research, and an excellent one at that. On top of that, the information she provided had helped cure me of this writer's block. Ever since I'd met her, the words were flowing like beer at a frat house kegger.

It didn't hurt, of course, that she was easy on the eye.

I shook my head and imagined the text of that Lovecraft book written in faded old dried human blood. Then I took another sip of my Algonquin cocktail—a rye, vermouth, and pineapple juice concoction. I winced at the strength of it. The blend of flavors played across my palate, and I could almost feel the alcohol being absorbed into my skin.

Alcohol had always had an immediate effect on me. I wasn't much of a drinker. At least prior to that wolf biting me. In my previous life, I was a lightweight who couldn't walk in a straight line when I was only a drink or two in. But ever since developing my enhanced strength and senses due to this werewolf blood in my veins, my tolerance level had increased. But I was still a novice when it came to handling alcohol.

And the drink helped to reduce the power of my enhanced senses. Not to mention the effect of dispelling some of my nervousness about seeing her.

That thing between Gail and me in the beehive was something else. I'd never been so forward with a woman in my life.

In retrospect, when I think about it, I might have been so bold with her because this was a strictly business relationship. She was on a celibate year.

I needed research help. And maybe some inspiration to keep that pen flowing.

But that was where it stopped. That was where it had to stop.

She might find me attractive, but I needed to respect her longer-term desire to remain celibate. That's the whole point of self-control, right? You need to have the discipline to not do something because it's the healthy and right thing to do, even if you desire it.

So respecting that was important.

But so too was the unnerving fact that I had been celibate—mostly unwillingly—for more than ten years.

When *was* the last time I'd had sex? It was the spring before I arrived in New York.

The spring of 2003.

Okay, this was ridiculous. I hated when it felt like I needed an abacus to count how many years it had been.

I hadn't been able to bring myself to be intimate with a woman because of the worry of what might happen if—

These rambling thoughts immediately stopped.

Gail was just outside the front door of the Algonquin.

I quickly took another sip of my drink and was putting it down on the coffee table in front of me when she appeared around the corner of the front entrance to the hotel.

She turned and spotted me immediately after she walked in. I heard her heart do a mini backflip that seemed to sync with what my own heart was doing.

Dammit, she was hot.

She was wearing a black, outrageously fuzzy sweater, almost a satire of feminine flounce, and an armload of spiked silver bracelets. I was most intrigued by the thigh-high boots she wore over her softly worn jeans. I hadn't seen her in heels yet, and I couldn't help but wonder if she had chosen them knowing she'd be standing near me.

I stood from the couch in the Algonquin lobby bar where I was sitting as she walked over to me.

She placed both of her hands on my shoulders, leaned in, and gave me a quick kiss on my right cheek.

It was a polite peck that lasted a mere millisecond, the kind you see friends in Europe offer one another without a second thought. But it took everything in me not to melt to the floor when her lips grazed the side of my cheek.

My legs felt like they were going to give out. The bones in my legs had turned into rubber. My cheek was tingling as if she had used Tiger Balm for lipstick. And there was another part of my lower region that seemed to replace that aforementioned lack of bone.

"Andrews," she grinned. "You look like a million bucks. You didn't have to dress up."

I reached up to touch where she had kissed me on the cheek, and I looked down at my front.

I was wearing a pair of jeans, a plain gray T-shirt, and a black blazer. It was one of the simple and casual yet professional "writer-look" outfits I wore when I wasn't sure whether or not to dress up for something.

"It is a…business meeting," I said. After the words left my mouth, I realized I was saying that mostly to remind myself.

For the briefest moment her face seemed to fall, and I sensed an air of disappointment. But she recovered quickly and the professional demeanor returned.

This *was* a business meeting. She was being polite and friendly.

And she was on a celibate year.

I invited her to sit down, and she took a spot on the couch where I'd been sitting. I shifted over and sat in the chair that was at a ninety-degree angle to the couch.

The waiter who had served me earlier appeared out of nowhere. At least, that was how it seemed to me because I had been so fixated on Gail.

"What can I get for you?"

"Oh," Gail said. "I haven't had a chance to glance at the menu." She turned to me. "What do you recommend?"

"Their vodka martini is legendary," I said, eying my nearly finished drink.

"Sounds good."

"Two vodka martinis, please. Three olives."

"Certainly," the waiter said, then moved off.

Gail looked at my drink sitting on the edge of the coffee table in front of her. "That's not a martini."

"No, it's a rye and vermouth mixture. One of their other house specialties. I like to try different ones."

She reached out for it. "May I?"

"Sure."

Lifting the glass, she took a quick sip from it. She didn't even wince in the slightest when she drank it. "That's nice," she said. "Sweet finish. The pineapple adds an intriguing touch."

How she could drink something that strong without recoiling was beyond me. I think I winced on her behalf just watching her sip it.

I looked down at the glass, and the slight residue of her lipstick on it reminded me of the feel of her lips on my cheek just moments ago. My cheek started to tingle again with the memory.

I reached for my glass, downed the last of the drink, and let my freak wince fly.

I needed to get my mind back to the business at hand: discussing my research needs.

Focus on that book. The one bound in human flesh. The one written in blood.

"I was so fascinated with the idea of that special *History of the Necronomicon* edition written in blood you told me about that I did a bit of research on the origin of the practice."

I began relaying some of the details of my research to her. I continued sharing until our drinks arrived. I took a long swallow of the martini and kept talking a mile a minute. I realized I might have been coming across like my salesman friend Buddy.

Nervous wasn't a big enough word for how I felt.

It had been bad enough thinking about it all day. But it was worse sitting across from her in that luxurious lobby.

My mind kept racing back to that afternoon. To the memory of being crammed into that small space with Gail, face-to-face with her, inhaling her delicious scent and the honey's sticky-sweet aroma. I'd almost lost control and leaned into her and kissed her.

When I had reached up to gently pluck the hair from her shoulder, I was shaking inside. I'd never done anything like that in my life. Never been so forward, so bold. If I hadn't had the excuse of doing it to help the entangled bee get out, I never would have done it.

But now I was entangled.

Not to mention tongue-tangled.

So, I reverted back to discussing the occult and the original excuse for seeing her again. It helped keep me distracted from the desire I felt when her eyes locked on mine.

And I kept talking.

"In modern use, the term *written in blood* has been referenced when talking about the reactive rather than proactive approach to drafting safety regulations. You'll hear terms such as 'safety standards are written in blood' in car manufacturing and air regulations. This is because the newly implemented rules result from horrific events that have cost people property, their lives, or both."

Damn. Those eyes. She was focused directly on me, politely attuned to what I was saying, but the look of intent focus in those gorgeous green eyes was also turning me on. It took everything in me to try to tune out the effect she was having on me, so I doubled down on the recitation of the facts I'd learned in my own research.

"The practice of writing in blood can be traced back to ancient Buddhist scriptures. Long texts, consisting of thousands, sometimes hundreds of thousands of Chinese characters, and even illustrations, were part of prolonged ritual practice. It was associated with self-sacrifice."

Instead of looking at her as I spewed these details, I tried to take in the activities of the other people in the bar, watch their movement, detect their unique scents. But that did no good. I couldn't tune out Gail's own scent, nor the hypnotic beat of her heart. I kept blathering on.

"Blood-written words were believed to sanctify and even animate the scriptural texts in a way that no regular ink could ever do.

"In ancient China, blood was considered a vital life-giving fluid. It was ultra-yang, representing the element of fire, the source of life, and creative power."

I paused to take another drink and gazed at her. Why did she have to look like that? Why was my heart doing backflips just looking at her? Despite the alcohol I had already consumed, I hadn't been able to dampen my senses all that much.

And I could tell she hadn't been surprised by the details I'd just shared with her.

Putting my martini glass down, I asked, "You already knew all that, didn't you?"

She nodded. "Most of it, yes."

"Then why were you letting me go on and on about it?"

A playful flicker lit up her eyes. "You were on a roll. I didn't want to stop you."

Slow your roll.

I had been trying to slow my roll, by talking shop, by focusing on the occult and the research and my book—speaking of which, I was making such good progress on the novel now and really *should* have been working on it rather than spending the evening with Gail.

But how could I resist? It seemed like time spent with her resulted in fuel and passion for writing. It was almost as if the heightened sexual desire she instilled in me resulted in the burning flow of words from my proverbial pen.

"But you have far more experience in this realm than I do. So tell me more," I said, "about the practice of blood in writing."

"Sure." She smiled, sipping from her own martini glass without taking her eyes off mine.

Combining that with the playful scent coming off her twisted my stomach into more knots than a pretzel factory. That look also caused a different part of my body to be the furthest thing from compact and curled up. I had to consciously focus to compel the wolf nature in me from leaping from the chair I was sitting in across from her and scooping her up in my arms.

"There's a book I occasionally stock in my store. A classic by Rudolf Steiner called *The Occult Significance of Blood*. It sheds some interesting insights into the use of blood, particularly in sacrifice. But blood has always been used for sacrifice. The Aztecs believed that the Gods sacrificed their own blood to create the universe and, in turn, offered their own blood as a thank-you. That's where the ritual of offering a warm and still-beating heart from a sacrificial live victim came from."

I picked up the powerful odor of shock and disgust from two older gentlemen in dark suits at a small table a few feet away from us. They must have overheard the topic of our discussion.

Glancing their way, I noticed the matching look of contempt for us.

"Whoops," Gail said, and I looked back at her to notice she had picked up on that too. "I suppose we should keep it down." She turned her head back toward me, and when our eyes met, I could tell she was on the brink of bursting into laughter.

I had to suppress my own outburst. I suddenly felt like we were a couple of friends being silly in church and trying not to laugh. That made me want to laugh that much louder.

What *was* it about this woman who brought out such intense emotions?

"Maybe," I said, biting my bottom lip to keep the laughter inside. "Maybe talking about such macabre details in a swanky place like this isn't the best idea."

Gail nodded, shuffled over on the love seat, and patted the spot next to her. "Slide on in here so we can discuss this without upsetting the high-end theatre crowd. I don't bite."

I moved from my chair to sit beside her. Very consciously, I tried to move in slow motion so that it wouldn't appear I'd been longing to sit close to her the entire night.

"Well, I can't promise I won't." I might have actually made a low growling sound from my throat.

Based on the increased pulse and the pheromone scent she was giving off, she definitely heard that.

She let out a playful purring sound in response. "If this wasn't a strictly professional relationship," she said quietly, "we could just take this conversation upstairs to your room. And then we could be as loud as we wanted."

I couldn't believe she was so forward. Her quickened heartbeat was clearly obvious to me, but based on the look she was giving me, I also couldn't be sure she couldn't hear the intensity of my heart beating in my chest. I could feel the pulse beat throbbing in my ears.

Based on my animal instincts and senses, there was no doubt that she was interested. But she'd shared this was to be a celibate year. I needed to respect that. I needed to respect her. Heck, as much as I desired her, I would gladly sit close to her and bask in that look she gave me that curled my toes. I could die a happy man with that face smiling at me the way she did.

And besides, I've never been one to make any sort of move when it came to women. Ever. Call it my Canadian upbringing, or call it my fear of overstepping my bounds. But I always let the woman make the first move.

Some alpha male I turned out to be. If only I was as alpha in human form as I was when I turned wolf.

"Yeah," I sighed. "Too bad this is strictly professional. Of course, we could always stay here and talk about something else."

"Like what?"

"Bees. I hear they're all the buzz lately."

She groaned and rolled her eyes. Of course, it didn't matter what she did with her eyes; I was hooked like a fish. When she rolled her eyes, my stomach did an outright flip-flop.

And the way her cute little nose wrinkled whenever I shared a horrible pun? It drove me insane.

"Good idea, changing the subject. It would allow us to just *bee* friends."

We both laughed aloud at that, perhaps a bit too loudly.

The grumpy couple at the other table turned abruptly, scowling, and made loud tsk noises in our direction. Then they grabbed their drinks and moved to a table farther away from us.

"Whoa," I said, "who pissed in their prune juice?"

Laughing, Gail said, "They look like they were born to be offended."

"Should I go apologize to them?" I asked.

"You can take the boy out of Canada, but you can't take the Canada out of the boy." She laughed. "Naw, leave Statler and Waldorf to stew in their misery. I'm glad they *buzzed* off."

I let out another burst of laughter when she used the names of the two cantankerous old men who consistently jeered at and heckled the performances of *The Muppet Show* from their balcony seats.

"You really need to *bee-hive* yourself," I said.

"*Wasp* on earth are you talking about? I'm sitting here minding my own *beeswax*."

We were laughing uncontrollably at the stupidest of jokes and a string of puns that had gone too far a long time ago. But the release of the tension felt incredible. If we hadn't been laughing, I think my head might have exploded.

"Okay," I finally said, out of breath. "Enough with the bee talk. I think we've *combed* through all the *sweetest* puns by this point."

She didn't laugh at that. I didn't even get an eyeroll.

"No more bee talk," she agreed. Then a mischievous grin came over her face. "Why don't we talk about the birds *and* the bees?"

"Mrs. Robinson, you're trying to seduce me." I paused, and the nervousness I was feeling would have made Dustin Hoffman's portrayal of Benjamin in that classic film look full of confidence. "Aren't you?"

Gail grinned at that reference. "Coo, coo, ca-choo," she said. "I may have been trying to do just that, actually."

Her phone vibrated on the table beside her martini.

She looked at it, then looked at me

"That's Isabeau, isn't it?" I asked.

"Yeah. She's checking in to make sure I sleep alone tonight."

"She's a good friend. She's looking out for you."

"Yes, she is." She picked up her phone without looking at it and stood up, slipping it into the back pocket of her jeans. "That text was perfect timing. We *should* call it a night. Because if I don't leave now, I swear I will break my vow of chastity all over you like an egg on its way to an omelet. And then I'd have to answer to Isabeau."

"And I'd have to worry about her coming after my balls with a rusty spoon," I joked, mimicking the defensive gesture of covering my crotch with my hands.

I stood up.

We faced one another.

Mark Leslie & Julie Strauss

I was reminded of standing so close to her earlier this afternoon and how intense it had felt.

Not to mention how hard it had been to pull myself away.

"I really enjoy our time together, Gail."

"Me too," she said.

"Have a good night," I said, leaning in to give her a hug. She moved into my arms for a warm embrace. I swear I felt intense tingling at every point of contact between us; there were hundreds of nerve endings across my body tearing around and screaming *Good Vibrations.*

The hug lasted a full beat, then another.

I wasn't willing to let her go just yet, and I squeezed a little harder. Breathing in the combination of the sandalwood and vanilla scent of her hair this close hypnotized me. Feeling her against me was even better than I had imagined. And I had imagined it a hell of a lot in the past several days.

She didn't let go either. Her own arms tightened a bit more.

Another beat passed.

"This is nice," I said.

"It is."

"See, a nice hug. Chastity intact. It's all good."

"I could stay like this all night."

"Me too. It's perfect."

"Yeah," she breathed. "Except there's this one problem."

"What's that?"

"Are you *sure* you're Canadian?"

142

"Why?"

"Because I didn't think Canadians carried guns."

"What?" I started to pull back from her, confused.

She let out a giggle and reached down with one hand on the back of my ass and pulled me back in tight against her, so my hardness pressed against her thigh.

"Oh," I said. "Yeah, that. I am *always* happy to see you. Ecstatic, even."

"Oh, don't worry, I can tell. But you know what would make *me* happy? Perhaps even ecstatic?"

"Tell me," I whispered into her ear a little more forcefully than I had intended.

She pulled her head back and looked up in my eyes, her breath hot on the top of my throat. "If I could stop wondering what it would feel like to kiss you."

I swallowed and licked my lips.

"I think that could be a—" I had been about to say *I think that could be arranged*, but her lips were against mine before I could finish.

Never had a kiss sent such an energetic bolt of lightning through me as that one did. I'm not sure how long we stood there, parted lips pressed together, our tongues dancing and flicking about in a parallel manner to the dance we'd played earlier in the day when we playfully teased one another by standing so close without touching.

All I remember is the kiss finally broke as we morphed from the explorative cavorting of our tongues into laughter after hearing the two cranky old farts complaining about the public display of affection taking place in the Algonquin lobby.

We then moved upstairs, and the minute we got inside my suite we resumed the kiss, standing right there inside the door.

This time there were no cranky old men to interrupt us. This kiss went on for an even longer time.

Breathlessly, Gail pulled back and said, "Okay, my neck is killing me here, Stretch. Let's say we go lie down?"

I nodded wordlessly.

"But first," she said, her eyes locking onto mine, "a lady needs to know she's safe when alone in a hotel room with a gentleman. There's still an unconfirmed rumor of a concealed weapon."

As she spoke, both of her hands traced a path from my shoulders, down my chest, lingering on my abs, then farther down, where she rubbed me with her palms.

"I'll need to ensure," she said, deftly unbuckling my belt and the button on my fly and unzipping my pants, "for my own safety, that there's no weapon, and you are, in fact, very happy to see me."

My heart jumped into my throat as she slid her hands beneath the elastic of my boxer shorts and took me in both hands.

We both gasped as she did this.

"Oh, Andrews," she said, still locking me in place with those eyes that kept me transfixed. "You are certainly packing a lot of heat here. We're definitely going to need to do something about that."

I nodded and swallowed. "Yes, we are."

"Which way is your bedroom?"

Without taking my eyes off hers—I don't think I could have done so if I tried, not that I wanted to—I gestured with a nod.

"Okay, then," she said, twisting her body to start moving in that direction, but keeping her eyes on mine, her right hand firmly locked on the evidence of my heightened desire. "Let's mosey on over in that direction." Walking backward, she pulled me by the cock toward the bedroom.

"Lead on, Macduff," I said, thinking about the words she'd used when we'd gone searching for a meal to sate our mutually ravenous pangs of hunger.

That hunger was, of course, nothing compared to just how intense my appetite was for her at that very moment.

She laughed. It was at once one of the most beautiful and most sensual sounds I had ever experienced.

Little did I know that just minutes later I would experience what would be the most sensual and incredible experience I had ever felt in my life.

.

Wednesday, May 25, 2011

Chapter Ten

GAIL

The least sensual sound a person can hear after the most incredible night of their life is the sound of a phone ringing at the crack of dawn. I have my phone set to 'do not disturb' at night, and the only exceptions on my contact list are Isabeau, my Uncle Albert, and my brother Ben. It sounds selfish, but I prefer to think of it as self-preservation. Not only do I not want to be accessible to robocalls or Len the Lizard at all hours of the day, but it also prevents certain negative influences (*cough*, my mother and most of my exes, *cough*) from reaching me when I'm trying to get my beauty sleep.

So a six a.m. call, naturally, startled me awake. It took a moment to place where I was. I looked down at the arm draped over my waist, holding my hand, and squeezed it gently before sliding out of bed.

"Hang on," I whispered to my brother when I picked up the phone. I ducked into Michael's bathroom and sat on the edge of the bathtub. "What's up?" I asked after I shut the door.

"Why are you acting so secretive?" Ben asked. "Is Jonathan still sleeping?"

"N-no. That is, I don't know what Jonathan is doing. Most likely, he is sleeping. Probably with someone else."

"Oh, shit," he said. "Not again."

"Mm," I agreed. Incredible how little I cared about Jonathan all of a sudden.

"So why are you whispering?"

I stretched my hands above my head and languished in the tingly soreness of my body but didn't reply. Still, Ben must have heard something in my silence.

"Are you kidding me?"

"Keep your voice down."

"I don't have to keep my voice down," he practically shouted. "I am alone in my apartment. Just like you should be."

"Joke's on you," I said. "I'm not even in my apartment."

He was silent on the other end of the line for a long time. "Why are you so dumb?" he finally said.

I blinked a few times. My brother was not usually unkind. He'd say that was my job in our relationship.

"I'm not dumb. I got rid of the guy I was being dumb about. Last night I spent the night with a really nice guy. For money."

"Excuse me?" he shouted.

"No, not like that." I struggled to contain my laugh. "I'm being paid to help him with research. But I'm at his place because he's amazing."

"You say that every time. And you get hurt every time. The men you like are jerks."

"Not this guy," I said. It was tough to speak quietly, because I legitimately wanted to screech my excitement. "He's *Canadian.*" I rolled the word around my mouth like a warm marble.

My brother sputtered a reply, probably something about global politics or sports teams or something else absolutely useless in real life, but I didn't really listen because I was holding the phone away from my ear. I could hear Michael cough and the bed shifting. Music wafted through the door; a treacly love song, so I knew he was awake.

"Gotta go," I whispered, interrupting some tirade about Canadians burning down the White House. Honestly, my brother is so in love with ancient history he sometimes forgets how to talk to living humans.

"Gail?" I heard a tapping on the bathroom door. "You okay?"

I opened the door and grinned at him standing buck-ass naked in front of me. His line yesterday about tearing someone open with their teeth made a bit more sense now. I wanted to eat him up.

I moved in close and kissed his neck. "Want to join me in a bath?" I asked.

Once again, his weapon came to life against me, and I stroked him gently while he talked.

"It's not big enough for two," he said, "But you take one."

"Without you?"

"I'll watch," he growled, and then my skin spontaneously combusted.

I flipped on the hot water and slid down into the tub while he rummaged around under the sink.

"I think I have some—I don't know. Bubble bath or something?"

"Ah," I grinned. "Evidence of an ex-girlfriend?"

He looked momentarily abashed and cleared his throat. "No. I just like a bath sometimes."

God*damn*. If I had any sense, I would jump out of this tub and run for my life.

He poured something from a bottle into the bathtub, and the heady scent of lavender filled the small room. I sighed and sank into the hot water, letting it soak my hair. When I came up for air, he was sitting on the edge of the tub, staring at me.

"Who were you talking to before I came in?" he asked. His hand dropped into the water, and he stroked my leg from the ankle to my knee.

"My brother," I said.

"You don't get along?"

"Why would you ask that?"

He shrugged, and his hand stopped moving on my leg. "Just a hunch," he said.

I bent and stretched my leg to fit it back into his hand. "Actually, we're really close. Although he's been annoyed with me lately."

"Why?" The hand started inching farther up, then back down to my ankle and over to my other leg. He got closer to my center each time he moved up, and my body agonized for him.

"Oh, I don't know." My breath was shallow. "You know how siblings are sometimes." I really was not in the mood to talk about my brother.

His fingers drifted up over my belly and up to my breasts, where he made lazy, slow circles around my nipples. His face looked serious, as if he was trying to memorize something. I arched my back up to fill his palms, but he kept a breath away from me. The light touch deliciously tortured me. I couldn't speak anymore, so I let my eyes drift closed and moaned a little bit. Finally, Michael's hand began its slow descent down my body again, and I gasped loudly. I clasped my hand around his forearm—my God, those forearms. They turned out to be everything I'd tingled over at the café.

"Come in here with me," I said.

He chuckled lazily, and I nearly fainted and drowned. "I already told you, the bath isn't big enough for both of us."

"That's what you think," I replied.

I stood up, stepped one foot out of the tub, placed my palms on his chest and pushed him gently. His eyes opened wide as he slid backward, and then he laughed and splashed a handful of lavender-scented water all over me and most of the bathroom.

"I never told you I ran track in college, did I? My thighs are made of iron."

I didn't think his eyes could go any wider, but they did when I said that. I stepped my foot over his other side and lowered myself onto him, tucking my heels against my butt, so we fit perfectly.

"My head's banging on the tile," he murmured into my chest, in between the gymnastics his tongue was working on my body.

I ran my hand up the back of his neck and held it against his head. "I don't want you to get hurt. Let me do all the work." He let his hands float on the surface of the water, and I began to rock, keeping my pace just as slow and methodical as he had when he moved his fingers against me.

Every time he tried to push harder, I pulled back a bit, tantalizing him the way he had done to me only minutes before. When I could see that it was too much for him, he reached his hands up and grabbed my waist, pulling me down hard against him. I crushed my mouth into his, and we crested the waves together.

*   *   *

"Can I wear this?" I grabbed a Rush concert T-shirt from a folded pile of laundry that appeared to be nothing but Rush concert T-shirts.

"You don't want to put on your own clothes?" he asked.

"Not if I— I mean, yes, sure, I'll put on my clothes. I wasn't sure if you wanted to do breakfast or—"

He stopped me midsentence with a deep kiss, putting an end to my awkward babbling. My hands dropped to my sides, and he pulled the shirt from me, ran it slowly up my back, and then only broke apart from the clinch to pull it over my head. His lips met mine again, and he continued kissing me as he pulled it over my wet hair, shoulders, and arms, and then he guided it ever so slowly over my breasts and belly. He wrapped his arms tightly around me again and growled into my ear. "I want you to stay."

When Michael took my hand and led me back into the bed, I ducked my nose into the fabric and inhaled deeply. The shirt was thick and soft and smelled just like him — musk and forest. He pulled me under the covers and then tucked them around me, exactly the way I love them — tight, but not too tight, just enough to make me feel covered. Safe.

Our bodies fit together like puzzle pieces, and I burrowed into his arms.

"How did you sleep?" he asked me.

"For the few hours you let me sleep, you mean?" I teased. "Fine. Great, actually. I'm not much of a sleeper, but I conked out last night. You?"

"Same," he said. "It surprised me."

"Why? Did you think I would snore?" I asked.

He paused. "It's been a while since I've actually slept with a woman."

"Oh, I bet," I said. "Women really hate the whole *tall, dark, and handsome* thing you have going on. Ew. It's so gross."

He laughed and kissed my forehead, pulling me in even tighter against him. "I just meant..." Another pause.

I stiffened. *Uh-oh.* Was this going to be the part where he revealed his criminal past? He was about to tell me that he was wanted for murder in every Canadian state. Not that I had any idea how many states there were in Canada. I would have to call my brother to find out. Hundreds, knowing my luck. Not only that, but he was probably some kind of thief.

Michael propped his elbow on the pillow and rested his head on his palm so he could look directly at me. I dragged my hand lazily up and down his back, figuring I might as well enjoy his velvety skin for a few more minutes before he ruined everything by telling me about his days of robbing graves, banks, and pet stores.

"You're not the only one who's been through a lot," he finally said. "I've had a hard time connecting with women for a while now."

"Is it because you have such shitty taste in music?"

His mouth dropped open, and he reached over me to pull the remote control off the nightstand. He then proceeded to turn the music up, and I clasped my hands over my ears. "I like a love song," he said.

"Does it have to be this love song?" I groaned. "Air Supply? It's so cheesy."

"Okay, sure. Let's do this. What's the best love song?"

"'The Bitch is Back' by Elton John," I replied promptly.

He grinned. "Wow. I see I've got my work cut out for me. By the time I am finished with you, I guarantee you'll love the weepiest, most romantic songs ever sung."

"I have no interest in that," I said, and I grabbed the remote out of his hand and pushed the arrow button. The next song was no better—a seventies power ballad with a wailing sax and a high-pitched singer to match. I buried my face in the pillow and groaned. "Don't you have anything sexy?"

He rolled his eyes. "Don't tell me you want a Barry White song? That's a little obvious, isn't it?"

"Give me your favorite non-obvious sexy song."

"Don't laugh."

"I won't laugh if it's not funny."

"Well-l," he said nervously, "The first time I…"

"Had sex?" I volunteered.

"No," he said. "The first time I had sex with someone I was in love with, we were listening to a Canadian band called the Barenaked Ladies."

I had to bite my lip really, really hard.

"And we heard this song called 'Hello City.'" He shrugged. "What can I say? It has certain associations for me."

"But is the song any good?"

He looked as if he was trying to decide what to tell me. "It's kind of silly."

"So is sex."

He didn't even laugh. Just nodded as if I'd spoken a profound truth. "Right. But also, there's this sort of punchy beat, and every now and then, there's a *womp-womp* of a trombone to remind you they really know what they're doing."

"Hunh," I said. I so badly wanted to make fun of his choice, but damn if he wasn't the hottest nerd I'd ever met.

"I can feel your disdain, and I don't care," he said. "What is your favorite song to make love to?"

I groaned. "Baby, I'm not talking about songs to make love to. I'm talking about songs to *fuck* to. I'm talking Nina Simone, Al Green. 'Crimson and Clover.'"

"Over and over?"

"There you go, Andrews. Join me on the dark side. We have great sex."

"I think we should test your theory," he said. He stopped the awful song currently playing. "Let's have a contest. Yours versus mine." He untangled his legs from mine and scooted back a few inches, so we lay parallel. "Get away from me."

"Where do you expect me to go?"

"I dare you not to touch me when I play my song," he said, clicking on the Barenaked Ladies.

Was this guy for real? He grinned at me from his pillow, and I hated how badly I wanted to kiss him.

"You gonna make it, Tough Lady?"

"If you get a hard-on, you'll touch me, so you lose." He scootched his hips back a little farther, and I couldn't help but laugh.

"What's your choice going to be?"

"'Smooth' by Santana," I said confidently. "I give you ten seconds, Andrews. You're gonna be all over me like honey on a hot biscuit."

He switched immediately to my song, threw the remote on the floor, and grabbed me in a rough embrace, rolling on top of me and kissing me so passionately I could hardly breathe.

I laughed again when our lips finally parted.

There was an awful lot of laughing happening when I was around this man. But I didn't trust it. All this happiness was starting to freak me out.

Chapter Eleven

MICHAEL
2:48 p.m.

"Twenty-four days," I murmured.

Then I shook my head, thumbed off the app I'd been looking at, and shoved the phone back in my pocket.

Thinking like this and doing the math was starting to freak me out.

Because I shouldn't be so obsessed.

I couldn't afford to be.

The app I'd been looking at was one I used to help me calculate when I was most likely to turn into my wolf self. While there was the occasional variation to the pattern, it usually happened when the moon was at least three-quarters full.

And I had just calculated, given that the moon would be at 78.2% on June 18th, that I had twenty-four days. Or, at least, twenty-four more nights with Gail.

But I had to stop myself from thinking like that.

Last night was good. Oh, who am I kidding? Last night was amazing. So was this morning. If I was completely honest with myself, I don't think I'd had sex as many times previously in my entire life as I'd had with Gail last night and through both the wee hours and the late hours of this morning.

I actually lost count. And one might only imagine I should have been keeping count. Particularly because it had been so long for me.

Eight dry years.

I had, of course, been purposely avoiding the opportunity any time it might have come up—however infrequently that happened—in the past. In the early days of trying to figure out the best way to live with my werewolf curse, I had been worried. Because one never truly knows, right? There's no guidebook, no manual on how to be a werewolf and how it worked. It was something I needed to learn.

And something I'd done entirely on my own.

There was an old television show I'd watched when I was young. *The Incredible Hulk*. I don't think I had seen it during its initial run, but rather when it was in syndication. The Hulk, of course, also appeared in the occasional Spider-Man comic over the years of my reading it. But it was that TV show I remembered most. Because whenever Dr. David Banner got angry, he would rage and morph into a huge, green-skinned, strong, and savage creature.

I would never forget the words that accompanied the opening to each episode.

Don't make me angry. You wouldn't like me when I'm angry.

In the early days, I worried that the wolf in me might also make itself known if my own emotions peaked in any way.

Such as having an orgasm.

In the handful of short-lived relationships I'd had over the past eight years, I completely avoided physical intimacy. Because I was too afraid that if I orgasmed, I might completely lose control of my human nature, and the beast would take over.

It wasn't that outrageous a thing to think about. Because every once in a while I would get angry or react to something, and I'd let out a growl that was far deeper, more guttural than I think any normal human could ever make.

So the beast, the animal, was there.

And the idea of losing control and morphing into a wolf while in the throes of passion terrified me.

Over the years, something happened that allowed me to forget the pain, torture, and extreme loss of control that came as I changed into a wolf. I'd figured I blocked it from my conscious mind because it was too unbearable for any sane person to live with.

But I still remember the utter terror of what it felt like to border on the edge of control.

And, in a parallel sense, that loss of control was somewhat similar to the experience of an orgasm. An orgasm was definitely an incredible feeling of ecstatic pleasure. And morphing into a wolf was extreme and outrageous pain. But the intensity was similar. And so was that terrifying loss of control.

Considering the number of times I had orgasmed with Gail in the past twenty-four hours, I could pretty much put *that* little theory to rest.

If the intensity of the extremes of pleasure and absolute loss of control we'd experienced didn't set off my metamorphosis, then nothing—other than the full moon, of course—could do that.

And so I'd caught myself checking that lunar calendar app and calculating how many more nights I could continue to have sex with Gail before the inevitable.

Because I needed to be far from her on the nights of the full moon. I had no consciousness of my time as a wolf and thus had no idea how my wolf self would react to waking up next to a female human.

And I could never risk that. I could never put Gail in that kind of danger. Come June eighteenth, I'd have to call an end to these naked romps under the sheets.

Or maybe I should consider calling it quits early.

After all, Gail was a scholar of the occult. She understood this paranormal stuff better than I did. It was why I needed her help with research. If I started to make myself scarce at the tip of each full moon, it wouldn't take long for her to figure out what was really going on.

Combine that with her obvious intuition and observation skills, and she'd be able to figure out the reason I knew so much. It was because I could overhear those phone conversations, even across a crowded and noisy café, even when it was whispered behind closed doors. And she'd figure out my extreme sense of smell too, either in my overreaction to subtle scents or when I had the knack of knowing a person's emotions.

No, she'd figure it out. She was too smart not to. And I was a horrible liar.

I already felt like she could see right through me.

It would likely be best to return to a platonic relationship. She had been the one, after all, to jokingly say she could never be a couple with someone with my particular taste in music.

We had both been sexually attracted to one another, and we'd had an exceptional time letting go of every single inhibition. And it was amazing. Incredible.

But she needed to get back to her celibate year.

And I needed to get back to being a blue-balls loner.

Not to mention, I needed to return to the front of that keyboard and continue bringing myself back on track with the novel that was already overdue.

I nodded my head and took in a deep breath.

It was settled. We couldn't keep doing what we'd done last night and this morning. We would need to return to the strictly business plan we originally established.

We needed to put some walls—some distance—between us.

So why, then, was I telling myself this while waiting in line to pick up tickets for tonight's performance of an off-Broadway show?

Tuesday, June 14, 2011

Chapter Twelve

GAIL

Isabeau had been chattering for the last hour, but I was having a hard time paying attention. Instead, I stared out the train window, watching our city fall away and the colorful countryside emerge.

"Have you heard that there's going to be an off-Broadway show about a battle between banshees and mermaids? It's supposed to be some feminist commentary, but I bet they'll just make it look like a wet T-shirt contest."

I handed her a book, hoping she wouldn't notice how distracted I was.

"Is it pronounced Wen-*deee*-go? Or Wen-*dih*-go?" She tucked both of her feet underneath her and flipped the pages without reading.

"It depends on the source," I told her, not looking up from the book I was pretending to read. "Every tribe has its own variation."

"All based in Algonquin family languages," she read aloud. "Don't you think it's interesting how neighboring communities develop similar folklore traditions?"

Algonquin.

I had dragged Isabeau on this field trip for several professional and private reasons, and it was unfair not to give her my full attention. But that word stuck in my head, and now I was lost.

Algonquin. A beautiful word, when I thought it over. And I had been thinking about that particular word almost every day for the last month. It was the combination that made it so delicious. A nice mix of hard consonant edges and soft, round vowels, ending in that pleasing, sonorous *nnnnn*. I muttered it to myself again, dragging out that last syllable as long as possible.

"Gail? Are you alive?"

I snapped back to attention. Iz was eyeing me coolly, a knowing quirk in her eyebrow.

"Sorry. Did you ask me something?"

"Tell me, why are we doing this? It seems like two people who just survived an apocalyptic bee attack should be watching over their store."

I sighed. "Is it weird that I kind of miss the bees?"

Her ebony face creased into a grimace. "Very. Those things could have hurt us if they wanted to."

"But they didn't want to," I said. "They just wanted to live their bee lives and make honey." I had, in fact, stopped lighting candles and incense when I opened the store, not wanting to diminish the rich honey scent that still lingered in the air.

"So, tell me why this conference is so important?"

"Professor Daanis is one of the preeminent Ojibwa scholars in the world. This talk about Wendigo folklore will educate us. When people come in looking for antlers for their Halloween costume, we can educate them about cultural appropriation and maybe teach them something real."

"Don't look at me. Stealing other cultures is white people shit."

"I know, I know. That's why I want to learn. But look at all the different lectures we can attend." I handed her the brochure and she looked through the long list of esteemed speakers.

She was quiet a moment, tapping her long nails— aubergine-colored today—on her phone. "And I suppose the fact that your mother is one of the speakers at this conference has nothing to do with why you invited me along?"

"A university conference on occult history makes perfect sense for us as owners of an occult store." I stared out the window again. "But we both know she's nicer to me when you're around."

"I like your mom," Isabeau said. "She has good vibes."

"I know you do. I love that about you." I reached across the little table separating us and squeezed her hand. "But you also didn't grow up with her."

Darina Sommers would find something to criticize about me the second I stepped off the train, and her criticism would not stop for the remainder of this week; that was one prediction I could make. She would point out that I was wasting my spiritual potential or serving the patriarchy through capitalism or some other nonsense. She'd compliment Isabeau, a woman who had the exact same job I had but who apparently made her life decisions from within her feminine genius. Or something like that. I was already exhausted.

I turned to watch the scenery moving quickly past the train window. The grays of Manhattan were changing to the saturated greens of Connecticut on our way to Rhode Island. This conference was one of my favorite annual excursions, and I was glad to have Isabeau with me this year. Soon we'd spot the vibrant red maples that I loved so much, and that sight alone would be worth the train fare. Just looking at them cheered me up. Every time I saw one, I took pictures and imagined living in a house painted crimson from top to bottom. I'd always wanted to bring a red maple leaf to a paint store and ask for an exact match. Better yet, maybe someday I'd collect thousands of leaves from the trees on my imagined property and glue them to the walls.

"I could live in Rhode Island," I announced. "If I bought a house here, I'd paint every single room that exact shade of red."

Isabeau stared at me like fish were growing out of my head. "What are you talking about?" she asked.

"Those trees," I pointed out the window. "You know how much I love them. I've read that red maple leaf has healing properties. We should stock it at the shop."

She stared at me for a long time, then crossed her arms. "You slept with him."

Damn.

Isabeau could straight up read my mind. It was spooky.

"With who?" I tried to use an innocent voice.

"Nope." She lifted her right index finger in the air, a teacher making a point to a very naughty student. "We aren't playing that game. That's why I've barely seen you all month, and you can't concentrate, and you're talking about crazy houses. You slept with that tall writer guy, didn't you?"

"His name is Michael."

We were at a stop, and passengers filed past our seats, oblivious to the war of wills happening in front of them.

"First of all, I don't see what his height has to do with—"

"I cannot believe I didn't figure this out," she interrupted. Now she stared out the window, even though there was nothing much to look at except a dull station.

I knew better than to try to pressure her into talking. Finally, she relented and turned back to me.

"You may as well tell me."

"What do you want to know?" Again, my voice was overly polite, and she narrowed her eyes. I was being cagey; she wanted to know everything. "Iz, let me just say this: he's good. He's *good*."

Her eyes hardened. "In bed?"

"No, that's not what I—well, yes. That too." I tried to force myself not to blush, but I could tell that it wasn't working. "What I meant was, he's a good man. A good person."

I saw her face soften, just a little bit, but she kept her stern expression. "Tell me."

"Okay, you know how I hate the smell of roses? Jonathan bought me roses all the time. At first, I thought he was a really chivalrous guy—he likes to act like a Hallmark hero who shows up to a date with a bouquet. And it's cute, and women are supposed to love getting flowers and all that shit. But after the sixth or seventh time I told him they make me sick to my stomach, I realized he was the opposite of chivalrous. He was just a guy with more dick in his personality than his pants."

"The writer is a good guy because Jonathan brought you the wrong flowers?"

"Don't be obtuse. And his name is Michael. I know you know that. You think he's like every other guy I've dated because he's tall. I'm telling you how he's different. A couple of nights ago, we were out for dinner, and I ordered a bowl of minestrone soup, and he said, 'Hang on, I think this place puts mushrooms in the minestrone soup.' I had mentioned that I don't like mushrooms once, just in passing, a few weeks ago, and he remembered. He lets me sleep in his T-shirts because they're softer than mine. He keeps the wine that I like in his fridge, even though he doesn't care for it. He asks me what I think of the books I'm reading and actually listens when I answer."

"And he's good in bed," she said. "I can tell by the way you won't share details. If he wasn't, I'd be hearing all about it."

I took a deep, slow breath and worked hard to steady my voice. "Yeah. That's pretty good."

"Oh, lordy." She groaned. "You are in trouble."

"That's what I'm saying—for once, I don't think I am."

"A few days away in Rhode Island seems like the perfect new boyfriend kind of getaway. So where is this Superman right now?"

"He thinks Superman is overrated. There's nothing interesting about a hero with superpowers. He's a big Spider-Man fan because the notion of a regular guy taking care of his neighborhood is the truest form of heroism." Her face hardened again, but I put up a hand before she could level me with one of her infamous zingers. "I know, I know. Not the point. He has a work thing."

"A work thing?"

"Yes, a work thing. Just like us."

"What, he can't sharpen his pencils in Rhode Island? There's not a thesaurus in the entire state?"

Now I was starting to get pissed off too. "He has an event. He speaks at things, appears on shows, does publicity. He's a very successful writer."

We sat in silence for the next half hour, and I itched in the misery of it. Iz and I rarely argued, but when we did, I felt like I was missing a lung. Finally, we heard the announcement that our stop was coming up, and we started gathering our things.

"I just don't want you to get hurt," she said quietly. "I know it's not about me, but try to put yourself in my place. Imagine watching your best friend's heart get broken over and over again. I feel so helpless."

"Maybe this one won't hurt," I said. "For once, I'm in it just for a good time. Pretty soon he'll finish his research, and we'll go our separate ways."

"My parents eloped after a month," she said. "My mom told me she thought they were just having a good time. They've been married thirty-five years."

"So I should marry him? That sounds like an extreme reaction to Jonathan cheating on me, but I trust your advice…"

She ignored me and continued her story.

"They both went to a Wham! concert with other dates. My dad had these glow sticks, and he broke them open and spread them all over his white shirt. My mom thought that was *totally bitchen*, so she asked for one and did the same. They got to talking, and they had the same favorite song. It was their wedding song."

"Iz, that is legit my dream love story. Imagine knowing he's the right one based on a song."

"Imagine marrying someone after knowing them a month," she said.

"Even weirder—imagine it lasting this long."

"How did your parents meet?"

"I have no idea. Uncle Albert was the only father figure I've ever had, and we're not even technically blood related. Mother has never once talked about my birth father." I lowered my voice to a dramatic whisper. "I suspect I'm a virgin birth."

She rolled her eyes. "Don't you dare try to copy my parents. They were stupid kids who got very lucky. You have a life."

I reached both of my hands across the little table. Iz looked at them for a brief moment and then put her palms on mine. "I do have a life," I said. "A really good one. And I'm just enjoying this guy while I can. If it turns into something, great. If not, I'll still be glad for my time with him. Really glad. Last night we were," I glanced around at the other passengers and whispered, "*you know*. And it's been good from the start, but last night it was so intense, I think I actually blacked out for a few seconds."

Her eyebrows went up a fraction. "Well, you know I'm going to need more details. But I see your mom standing there on the platform, so I guess I'll have to wait until we're alone in the hotel room?"

I looked out the window and saw my mother standing there, her salt-and-pepper hair spilling down to her waist, her skirts so voluminous that they rustled every time a passenger walked by. Despite the flowing madness of her crazy clothes, she held her head as erect as a ballet dancer, and her steely black eyes had already locked on me. I smiled and waved, but she only nodded in return. I wished I had the kind of mom I could talk to about my new boyfriend. Not that he was a boyfriend. I wished she was the type of mom who would ask to see pictures of him and agree that he was very handsome. She'd never been all that interested in my love life, and the few that she'd met, she'd nearly reduced to tears. Fortunately, I had Iz, who would gossip with me for hours.

"I promise I'll give you all the details you want. I have big details. Huge." I held my hands out, palms facing each other, and waggled my eyebrows lasciviously. That finally got her to laugh. "But first, we get to go learn about ancient cannibals."

"Wait—what? Wendigos are cannibals?"

"I wasn't talking about Wendigos," I said, darting a glance at my mother. "But yes. We'll learn about them too."

I took a deep breath and ran my hand over my hair, trying to smooth it to a decent style before her critical gaze, and I forced a smile so phony I could practically taste blood on my lips.

Friday, June 17, 2011

Chapter Thirteen

MICHAEL
5:26 a.m.

I woke up naked in a pool of blood.

"Not again," I whispered. And with the words came the taste of that blood on my tongue and lips.

A man cannot destroy the savage in him by denying its impulses. The only way to get rid of a temptation is to yield to it.

I'm not sure why those words from Robert Louis Stevenson's *The Strange Case of Dr. Jekyll and Mr. Hyde* flashed through my mind. Apart from the fact I was coated in rabbit blood. That wasn't a surprise. My alter ego often hunted, killed, and consumed rabbits.

What surprised me though was there was more than rabbit blood coating the ground and leaves where I woke up.

The blood was from at least two other species.

When it came to rabbit blood, I was intimately familiar with that. The second scent I was able to deduce was the blood of a raccoon. I can't recall having ever killed a raccoon before. Central Park had its fair share of them, but they were vicious little creatures, especially if they carried rabies. But I couldn't detect the bitter scent of rabies in the blood.

It took me another minute to determine what the third blood type was.

A coyote.

Those were exceptionally rare in this park.

Not for the first time since living with this lycanthropic curse, I wondered what the heck I had gotten myself into the previous night when prowling around on all fours.

I didn't even have to use my sense of scent to track down the carcasses of the three animals whose blood I was soaking in. Because they were all there. Plainly visible. The rabbit looked like it had been eaten; I'd found plenty of rabbit carcasses over the years and knew what one my wolf self had picked clean looked like.

But the raccoon and the coyote hadn't been eaten.

They had been ravaged and violently torn apart.

As I looked at the severed pieces of their bodies, I felt like I was looking at a scene of the aftermath of a *Texas Chainsaw Massacre*-style slasher film.

I gagged and almost threw up on the forest floor. But I didn't. Because, sadly, this was the third day in the past week that I'd woken up to this now-familiar scene.

Before this transition, my wolf self had never done anything like this.

And I recognized it as a crime of passion.

I'd conducted enough research into murder crime scenes for the mysteries I wrote to know how detectives could determine crimes of opportunity versus crimes of passion. Victims with dozens of stab wounds, for example, were evidence of a very personal attack, likely fueled by anger or some other intense emotion.

This made me wonder if part of my human emotions were seeping into the wolf.

I was, after all, completely pissed with the fact that, despite how close we had been—having spent every single night together since the first night we'd had sex— I'd had to bail on Gail.

Not to mention how angry I was that I'd let myself get that close to anyone.

How could I possibly have an actual relationship with a woman when I had to disappear for ten days every single month?

I hated myself for purposely avoiding Gail since June tenth. And I hated myself for lying to Gail. Particularly because, when I had told her I was booked to go away on an out-of-town trip for an author event, I felt like she could see right through my lie.

But worse than that, I smelled the immediate instinctual hurt she projected while I was telling her about my trip.

She had been lied to and cheated on before. I was likely just the latest in a string of bad choices with the wrong men.

I hated myself for causing that hurt. And for believing that I could ever have a normal life, a normal relationship with someone.

All that repressed emotion, that unresolved tension and anger at myself and my situation, was obviously coming out when I was in full animal form.

This couldn't keep happening.

I needed to put a stop to this. There was no way I could be with Gail.

As I was scrambling through the woods to find the spot where I'd hidden a stash of clothes, I resolved to not call or text her.

While pretending to be away, I regularly texted lies about where I was or what I was doing. But that all had to end.

I would drop the charade that I was out of town and tell her I was coming clean with her. I'd tell her I'd been using her for research for my book and no longer wanted to see her. The sex was great, but I got what I needed from her, and it was time to move on.

* * *

1:27 p.m.

"Excellent choice," Gail said as she rang in the purchase for the exquisitely matching goth couple she was serving.

I had to admit, this pair of goth teens had nailed their outfits and makeup. Though they were a male and female couple—something I could tell from their scents—they looked identical and could easily have been mistaken for twins if it wasn't for the fact the two had openly made out with one another when Gail had popped into the back room to retrieve a box for their purchase.

The goth couple had come in just a minute after I'd showed up at Gail's shop. I should have called or texted her—that's what the kids do nowadays, isn't it? But I couldn't do that to her. It felt like too mean of a thing to do. Too impersonal. She deserved better than that.

Gail had, of course, been surprised to see me.

Along with that surprise came warmth and a sense of pure pleasure from her. That gave me pause about addressing this, and I was immediately kicking myself for deciding to do this in person.

"You're back?!" she said. It was a statement and a question. "I thought you weren't back until the twenty-first."

"Yeah, there was a shipment issue for the last two bookstores on the journey. They didn't have enough stock, so the signings were called off."

When I'd come up with the lie about talks and book signings that would take me out of town, I had counted on the fact that Gail knew very little about the book industry. It was rare for publicists to set up a book tour—even a mini one—nine months after a book's release. Publishers usually focused all their energy and resources on propping up books during the first month of its release. They might get behind arranging events for an author outside that "new release" phase if the author was already traveling to a region and could make time in their schedule to include a bookstore stop or two along the way.

If Gail questioned that, I had planned to use the excuse that the publisher was doing it to play off the hype of the forthcoming movie tie-in. The layers of deception I'd already concocted were easy. I did, after all, make up shit for a living. But I had also shocked myself at how easily I'd been able to compound lie after lie, piling them up like a beaver piling up sticks to create a dam.

Only, it felt more to me like I was building a dam as well as damning any hope of a decent and honest relationship with a woman whose company I truly enjoyed.

I realized what I had just done. I'd lied again. I'd perpetuated the initial lie with another new one instead of using that opportunity to come clean with her.

I never actually left town was what I had intended to say to her. *I lied to you. I've been here the whole time. And the reason I lied is I didn't want to see you anymore.*

But I didn't. Instead, I manufactured another tale.

And that was when the goth couple had come into the shop, interrupting any further discussion. Gail turned to greet and serve them. I'd known the challenge she and Isabeau faced with the recent bee catastrophe repairs and all the lost inventory in the shop. She needed every sale she could get.

Watching her interact with them, I could tell they were prime for an easy upsell. And knowing Gail's intuitive nature and the way she read people, I figured she could pick up on that too.

Considering how desperately in need of any extra sales her shop was, I was shocked to watch her serve the couple's needs without ever using the leverage she could have pulled off effortlessly. She helped them, answered a slew of their questions, and complimented them on their on-point matching outfits. She even shared that she recognized that their look seemed to be a nod to the look and style of Peter Murphy, the lead singer of Bauhaus, the band often attributed with the start of the modern goth culture movement.

Watching her interact with customers was a truly wonderful experience. I realized I'd never seen her in her element. She was so in control, so in the groove, so masterful in her approach. I had to catch myself because I realized I was practically swooning while watching this brilliant and gorgeous woman work.

Why the heck did I want to break this off?

What the hell was wrong with me?

She wished the goth couple well as they headed out the door and turned back to me.

The smile on her face melted my heart.

"So," she said, walking slowly toward me, "you're back early. Maybe we could catch *The Green Lantern*. It opens tonight. I know it's not Spider-Man, your favorite superhero, but it does star Ryan Reynolds, and he's Canadian."

She placed both hands on my chest, and I swear I felt a tingling. Seeing her smile, smelling her enthusiasm for doing something as mundane as seeing a movie with me, and feeling the electric spark of her touch was too damn much.

I am, after all, a mere mortal.

I couldn't do confrontation on the best of days. And being presented with this compassion, thoughtfulness, and just plain sexiness pushed me even further from the ability to speak the words I had come to her shop to say.

Before I could say anything, the front door opened and a middle-aged white woman with sunglasses nestled above her bangs walked in. Her blonde hair was tied into a long and thick rope-like braid that cascaded in front of her right shoulder and ended mid-breast of a light blue zip-up hoodie.

The scent coming off this woman was a curious mix of nervousness and excitement. She had never come into a shop like this; that much was clear. But she'd come with a sense of wonder and hope, as if she was here to do research.

I could picture the minivan she drove parked out on the street and got the sense she had driven in after dropping her kids off at a nearby soccer tournament.

Gail excused herself and walked back toward the door.

"Welcome to Enchanting Magic. I'm Gail, one of the co-owners of this shop. How can I help you?"

"Well," the woman said, and her voice was filled with the trepidation and hope I detected in her scent. "I'm not sure if you can help me. But I just found out something about my ancestors that I'd like to learn more about."

"Oh," Gail said, clapping her hands together. "I do love a good challenge. Hit me."

The woman, it turned out, had been adopted. Just recently, she came upon the details about her birth mother. And part of the woman's legacy was that she was a descendant of one of the thirty witches found guilty during the Salem witch trials.

She was worried that this meant there was something inherently wrong with her, that she might be some sort of devil spawn and might need some kind of potion or spell to help purify her soul.

There was nothing to sell this woman. And yet I watched Gail spend well over an hour with her, sharing some insights and history about the tragic events of Massachusetts in the 1690s.

She also relayed the origins of Wicca and Neo-Druidism, the more modern pagan offshoots derived from nineteenth century Romanticism and, earlier than that, Renaissance magic.

Gail explained the ties between artistic, literary, and intellectual movements; to a spiritual movement that promoted the cultivation of honorable relationships with the physical landscapes, the flora, the fauna, the people, and with nature deities, and the spirits of place. She relayed the importance of divinity in nature. She shared how, prior to the Christian era, witches were honored and loved for centuries. Witches were consulted for relief in sickness, counsel in times of trouble, and involved in highly sought-after benevolent fertility-related rituals.

By the time Gail was finished with the woman, I sensed the incredible amount of relief coming off her. The woman had walked in fearful, nervous, and embarrassed about her ancestry. But by the time she left, she was feeling assured and even proud of who she was.

I'd watched Gail in action not as a salesperson nor as merely a scholar familiar with the occult. She was almost more of an effective and empathic therapist.

It made me realize that, instead of continuing to lie to her or try to break things off, maybe I could figure out a way to tell her the truth about who and what I was.

After all, she might be one of the only people to actually believe me. And she might be the best person to help me understand more about my wolfish nature.

But I wasn't sure how to do that yet. For now, it was easier for me to just go with the string of lies I had originally set up. Until I could figure out the best way to relay this information to her.

I still had three more days left of turning into a wolf. So I knew I wouldn't be able to see that movie with her tonight.

"Listen," I said. "I just came to let you know I'm back in town. And it was really good to see you. It was particularly fun to watch you at work. You're damn good at what you do. But I'm not going to be able to go to that movie tonight, fun as that sounds. I was unable to get any useful writing done during this mini book tour. I'm behind again, and I need to spend every waking moment digging into the book and getting things back on track."

It was a weak excuse. But it was the best I could come up with on the spot.

I sensed her disappointment, but her sadness over me having to say no to tonight's plan morphed into an odor tinged with suspicion.

"You came all the way here just to tell me you're back, but you can't hang out?"

"I missed you," I said. "Yeah, I have a ton of writing to catch up on, but I missed you and wanted to see you."

The scent of suspicion was replaced with that same warmth and spontaneous joy I'd smelled on her when I had first stepped into the shop.

She again placed her hands on my chest and kissed me gently on the lips. "Off you go, Shakespeare. Get that quill in your hand and get that writing done. I'll be here when you're all caught up."

As I walked out the door, the taste of her strong on my lips, I was reminded that I was deceiving someone I had grown to truly care about.

And I'd better come up with a way to explain my wolfish nature to her so I could stop making up this growing pack of lies. Especially since I doubted I would be able to keep this deception going for much longer.

I owed it to Gail to stop lying and tell her the truth.

She deserved nothing less.

Monday, July 4, 2011

Chapter Fourteen

GAIL

"I deserve so much more than this," Ben muttered.

"What more do you want?" I said. "We're in a prime fireworks viewing spot. I got here early enough to get us great seats. We have an amazing picnic." I indicated the spread of food arrayed on the blanket at our feet—meats and cheeses and crusty bread and grapes. "And you get the pleasure of my company. Which, as you complain about almost constantly, you don't get enough of."

I paused my lecture when a woman walked over our blanket, stepped on the corner of it, and didn't apologize. She didn't make eye contact, and normally I would have chalked it up to typical New Yorker behavior. But something about her stride—the way mine was the only blanket she stepped on in a sea of colorful cloths laid out across Roosevelt Island—made it feel intentional. She looked vaguely familiar, and I tried to place her as she walked away. I dragged my eyes back to my brother.

"Ben, can you please stop pouting? It's embarrassing."

"What's embarrassing is that I've been trying to talk to you for ages, and you can't seem to make time for me."

"We're here now, and you have my full attention. What do you want to talk about?"

"We need some time alone. When I said I wanted to see you, I meant just you. Not you and the beefcake of the month." He jerked his chin in the direction of the empty folding chair next to me.

"He's not a beef—" I started to argue, but then I saw Michael approaching and jumped out of my chair.

Suddenly I regretted this outing even more than Ben because I wanted nothing more than to be alone with Michael in a very private room. Any room. A broom closet would have made me happy. Right at that moment, I didn't want to share him with another soul.

He sauntered across the park toward us, a slight smile on his face, dressed in chinos and a denim button-up. Sleeves rolled to the elbow, naturally, because he was still a secret government assassin, out to end me. I was almost certain of it. Why did he always look so delicious? There was nothing remotely interesting about a man in chinos and a button-up. Most of the men in the country were wearing the exact same thing at this very moment. But Michael's clothes always looked like they had been custom tailored and stitched right onto his body. Even in the sweltering early summer heat, he looked cool and comfortable. His shirt stretched across his broad shoulders and nipped in at his waist, and his pants curved over his ass and showed off the bulge of his—

"Get your tongue back in your mouth." My brother interrupted my casual objectification with a laugh.

I waved so Michael would spot us, and he nodded and grinned back at me.

Michael gave me a hug and quick peck on my cheek. I could tell that he wanted to do way more than that when his hands clenched the fabric at my waist, but he pulled back and held his hand out to my brother.

"You must be Ben," he said. "Michael Andrews. Nice to meet you."

Ben stood up, and his polite smile didn't hide his cool appraisal. His eyes traveled from Michael's head to his toes and then back up again. He had slowly reached out his hand to meet Michael's handshake when their eyes met, and I saw my brother's eyes narrow.

"Benjamin Sommers," he said, his voice oddly locked.

"I've heard so much about you," Michael said.

Ben didn't bother replying with one of those usual remarks a person makes when someone says that. He didn't bother with a *Same here!* Or *I hope it was all good!* Or *Don't believe anything she said!* Even for my brother, it was awkward.

Michael, however, didn't seem to notice the absence of a return cliché. He pulled a bottle out of the messenger bag he wore over his shoulder. "Gail told me she'd manage the picnic. But I passed my favorite wine shop on the way here, and I remembered she told me you love French champagne, so I stopped in to pick this up. I hear this vintage is great, and I've been eager to try it."

Ben didn't take the proffered bottle or make a move, so I replied for him. "What a great idea!" I exclaimed, a little too eagerly. "It's a perfect night for something bubbly."

"That's what I thought," Michael said, and he turned his attention back to me and ran his eyes over my new outfit. "You look especially lovely tonight."

"You like?" I teased, twirling the skirt of my sundress like a five-year-old and tingling in the glow of his admiring stare. "I decided to dress up as a pretty girl."

"A pretty girl who wears black dresses and combat boots?" he said.

"Well, come on. I got a new outfit. Not a new personality."

We settled into our chairs, and Michael reached over and took my hand. I saw Ben's eyes narrow again.

Stop it! I mouthed. He was taking his protective older brother role a bit too far this time.

"So, Ben," Michael said, "Gail tells me you teach Cultural Anthropology. That sounds fascinating. How did you get into that field of work?"

"How does anyone get into any field of work?" my brother replied, his voice acidic. "I was interested; I studied it. Here we are."

"Yes, Ben, everyone knows how school works," I snapped. "That's not what he asked."

Michael didn't seem to notice our rudeness. He pulled three plastic champagne glasses out of his bag and cut the foil off the bottle cap. "I've always thought the best and worst parts of anthropology are that every step leads you to a new mystery," he continued. "It's the ultimate investigation, isn't it? I would think that every time you learn something, you have fifty new questions. And since, by definition, there is no one to answer your questions, you have to keep digging. Or you get to keep digging, depending on how you see your work."

There were very few ways to bewitch my brother, but Michael had landed on the one method that guaranteed success: think deeply about an intangible subject. My brother would take this kernel and talk all night. Michael was a genius. I turned to Ben, expecting him to match my enthusiasm, but to my surprise his face remained stony. I felt my wide grin falter.

"You've both written books," I announced. I was starting to stab around for random subjects they had in common as if that could save us from the awkwardness.

"Oh, really? What do you write?" Michael asked, his voice still placid.

"Academic books," Ben replied. "Nothing you would have seen."

"Probably not." Michael grinned at me when he said this. "I spend most of my time in the horror section of the bookstore. But I do love reading nonfiction. That's how Gail and I met—maybe she told you?" He picked up my hand and sent electric shocks through me when he absentmindedly stroked my palm with his thumb. "I'm in the middle of some heavy-duty research."

"Yes, I heard," Ben said, condescension dripping from his mouth. "How convenient that you just happened to find my sister."

"I lucked out," Michael agreed as if Ben was complimenting him.

"We both did," I said.

"Why *you*, Gail?" Ben turned his narrowed eyes on me. "Of all the people in New York City, don't you think it's odd that he came to you?"

"No, I don't." My falsely cheerful tone had disappeared. "Michael's the best at what he does, and his publisher asked me for help because I'm the best at what I do. It's not hard to understand."

"Excuse me." Michael stood up. "This food looks marvelous, and I'm hungry. I saw a washroom back there, so I'm going to go clean up before we eat."

He ambled away, hands in his pockets, looking like he was enjoying a garden party with the Queen, not watching two petulant adult siblings sling jabs at each other across a picnic blanket.

As soon as Michael was out of earshot, we turned to each other and hissed accusations.

"Gail, are you *out* of your *mind*?

"Ben, what the *fuck*?"

We stared at each other for a full minute, and I could not remember ever seeing that kind of vitriol on my brother's face before.

"Way to go. I've spent the last two months telling him how close we are, how well we get along, how you're the nicest guy I know, and you've known him for all of fifteen minutes and already proven me wrong on all counts."

We were standing up, though I didn't remember leaping to my feet to yell at him. A vein stood out on his temple, and his fists were clenched at his side.

"You don't have a clue what you've gotten yourself into," he said.

"I knew I shouldn't have introduced you."

"Oh, no, you absolutely should have introduced me. I only wish you'd have introduced me months ago. This is catastrophic."

"You can't stand it that I'm having a good time for once in my life, can you? It's no fun for you if your sister actually gets her life together."

He let his breath out in a long, slow exhale and looked up at the sky as if someone up there could provide him with answers. "Gail, this has nothing to do with whatever good time you think you're having. Which will end, by the way. You can't see it yet, but this good time will end."

"I think you have been spending too much time with Mom."

"Why would you say that?"

"Because you sound just like her. You're critical, judgmental of my choices, and rude to people I love."

"*Love*? Two months in with this guy, and you already think you love him?"

"That's not what I said." Though I realized right away that it was exactly what I had said. The words had slipped out of my mouth so easily. I made a mental note to examine that statement later. For now, I had a fight to win. "I mean anything I even remotely like. Mom is never satisfied, and frankly, neither are you. Lately everything I say pisses you off." I brushed away the angry tears that had suddenly filled my eyes. "I don't know why you're so mad at everyone all the time."

Ben hesitated, but then his face softened, and he took my hands in his and pulled me in to him. "This is what I wanted to talk to you about," he said. "I'm worried about you, and we need to talk about why. It's a long story."

"What's a long story?"

"The time I've been spending with Mom, I've learned a lot of things about our family," he said. He opened his mouth to continue, but his eyes darted to something behind me, and coldness descended over his face again. "He's back," Ben said flatly.

"Tell me." I yanked on his hands so he wouldn't pull away from me. "Ben, tell me what you are talking about."

He gripped me so tightly that my hands tingled. "Gail. You are in grave danger," he whispered.

"Grave danger?" I laughed. "What on earth does—"

But my brother walked away without another word.

Before I could call out for him to stop or ask another question, Michael rejoined me. I turned to look at him, and his smile was faint.

"Everything okay?" he asked.

"Fine," I said shortly. "I'm...I'm sorry, Andrews. My brother is—well, I don't know what's gotten into him lately. He's not usually so melodramatic."

"I do." Michael pulled me to his side, though he didn't kiss me. "He loves you. He knows what you've dealt with, and he's worried. It's natural for him not to like me."

"That's the part I can't figure out," I said. "You're so alike. I thought for sure you'd hit it off and go off on some random topic of conversation, and I'd sit here alone all night."

"I guess I'll have to earn his trust. I'm willing to try." His arm was firm around my waist—firmer, I thought, than it really needed to be. His eyes kept roving over my head, checking out the crowd.

"He's not coming back," I reassured him. "You won't have a chance to earn his trust tonight."

Michael looked back down at me and seemed to make a decision. "Do you want to leave?"

"But what about the fireworks? And we haven't even eaten."

"We'll pack it up and eat at my place," he said. "It's not as great a view, but we can go to the roof and watch the fireworks."

"Come on, Michael," I said. "You're not going to let my brother ruin our night, are you?"

"It's not just him." He turned to face me. "I think I just saw someone who recognized me. I'm not sure."

"A fan? Isn't that a good thing?"

"Usually it is, yes. But this one is different. I think she may be...off, somehow? I don't know. But I'm not comfortable."

"She can't possibly be bigger than you, Andrews," I said, trying to tease him into a better mood. "I'm sure there's nothing to worry about."

"I don't like it," he said. "Let's go. I promise I'll make it up to you."

By that point, I was sick being treated like a damsel in distress. All of the men in my life needed to stop swinging their dicks around and let me make my own decisions. But something in Michael's eyes made my blood run cold, and I gathered up the food I had laid out without any more questions.

* * *

"Not that it matters, but I have told everyone that you are the best lover I've ever had. I'm not sure why you decided to prove me wrong." I brought the ice pack up to my forehead and winced when it touched the lump that was already turning purple.

Michael looked away from his reflection in the mirror, where he was dabbing blood off the gash just under his right eye. "Everyone?"

"Literally everyone. I told my mail carrier. I brag about it every day. How our sex is so good, the neighbors have orgasms. Now I guess I need to admit it was all a lie?"

He patted a bandage over his cut and sat across from me on the bed. "I hardly think this makes *all* of it a lie," he said, taking the ice pack from me and looking at my forehead.

"Tell me the truth, Andrews. Are you sleeping with anyone else?"

His mouth dropped open. "No! Why are you asking that?"

"Because my brother trusts everyone, and he doesn't trust you. Because you got weird at the park, and I think maybe you saw an ex-lover. Or a current lover. Or, I don't know, your wife? Are you married? I've never even asked. And because now we can't even seem to fuck, and that is our thing, Andrews. We're practically the world champs of fucking. But we tried tonight, and now you're bleeding and I'm seeing double. Something is wrong."

"Wow," he said. "Okay. First of all, your brother is protective of you. I have nothing but respect for that. Second, I've never been married. Third, a few months ago, I met a strange woman who seemed like a stalker. She came on to me and was creepy when I turned her down. I could have sworn I sme— I saw her at the park tonight, and all I could think was what if she came after you? I wanted to leave. As for the making love—"

I bit back a smile when he said this. I secretly loved saying the f-word in front of him, mainly because he refused to refer to the act as anything besides *making love*.

"I'm just tired. I've been working too much."

"Do you think we should go to urgent care and have these injuries checked out? Your cut looks deep. You might need stitches," I said, gently touching his cheek below the bandage.

"Nah," he said. "I've had way worse injuries. This'll heal."

"Well, I don't want to go either," I said. "It will be full of drunk tourists with homemade fireworks burns. Going in there and admitting I got injured while attempting to have sex would be humiliating. Why is your skull so hard?"

"Why is yours so spiky?"

We stared at each other for a moment, then laughed.

"Well, let's just admit tonight's not the night for fireworks," he said, and he pulled me into him.

We settled back on his pillows. I rested my head on his chest, closed my eyes, and let my breathing match his.

After a while, he spoke. "Gail?"

"Mmm," I said, already drifting off.

"Will you spend the night with me?"

"Of course." I lifted my head to look at him. "I always stay the night with you."

"No, I know, when we are, you know. Doing things." I smiled at his sudden, inexplicable shyness. "This night has been kind of a bust. But I want you to stay anyway. I just want to be with you."

"I want to be with you too," I said, and I buried myself deeper into him. I had just drifted off when I heard him speak again.

"There is no one else, Gail. I don't want anyone else. I only want you."

I was in that floating part of the night, awake enough to barely register his words, not awake enough to answer him. But it seemed impossible that he couldn't feel my heart pounding inside my chest, up against his. I couldn't tell if I was answering him out loud or just dreaming the words, but I heard my response clearly.

I only want you too.

Wednesday, September 28, 2011

Chapter Fifteen

MICHAEL
5:15 p.m.

"I only want Remoudou," Gail said. "That's my favorite."

This was our first time shopping together—not to mention my first experience picking up groceries with anyone else—and I was surprised at how unique and domesticated the experience felt.

Gail was in it to win it, approaching this mundane task with the zest and intentness of a wedding planner. It was as if she was competing for a segment on *MasterChef* instead of planning for a picnic in Central Park. The whole time we'd been in this high-end grocery store she'd jumped into project manager mode. She was rather cute when she got this serious and determined.

"As you wish," I said. But she didn't pick up on my nod to *The Princess Bride*. She was deep in the cheese zone as part of this planning for our picnic.

"And maybe grab some Danish Blue. Did you like the brunost? It was the Scandinavian cheese I brought to the July Fourth picnic? That caramelized one that goes well on a pizzelle with a bit of jam."

"A pizzelle?"

"Those little thin sweet Italian waffle cookies."

"Ah. Yes. Those were delicious."

Of course, I didn't get to try them at the Fourth of July picnic itself. That whole thing was called off early. I tried most of the amazing foods Gail had prepared later on that night at my place. The evening turned out okay in the end, but it was pretty tense for a while.

It didn't help that Gail had accused me of sleeping with someone else. And I suppose that *would* have been the perfect opportunity to tell her the truth about my absence. But something about her brother's hostility toward me gave me pause.

I'd sensed his fear and hatred for me from several meters away, even as I approached the two of them that day. And I kept getting mixed messages from Ben. Part of him liked me and appreciated the gesture of the champagne I'd brought, the discussion about his work. Those emotions were there, but he kept them closely locked down and didn't let them show. Ben kept returning to the anger, the bitter fear he had about me. The odor of it in the air between us was so thick I could practically taste it.

It was as if Ben was sensing something about me. Like he knew I'd already lied to her. That it was inevitable I would hurt Gail.

So, that night, after we'd made up and snuggled together, the last thing I wanted to do was bring up my wolfish nature. I suppose I just wanted to hold her in my arms and pretend that everything would be all right.

I was about as good at confrontation as a feather would be at cutting steel. So I let it go, and figured I'd bring it up another day.

That day didn't come. Naturally.

"And maybe some Añejo cheese too."

"Pardon?" She'd been speaking to me, and I had been in wandering-mind mode.

"Añejo. It's a Mexican cheese. It'll be perfect for crumbling over our salad. And maybe also see if they have—"

"Cheddar?"

She paused and looked at me like I had three heads. "Cheddar?"

"Yeah. Good old Ontario cheddar."

"You're kidding, right? Why not just get some saltines and a can of Easy Cheese?"

"It's a taste of home for me."

"Okay, we'll include a Canadian cheese. But let's make it Oka. That's from Quebec. And Quebec is right beside Ontario…isn't it?"

She'd said that to be funny, and it would have been obvious even if I couldn't smell the mirth coming off her. I often made fun of how little she knew about Canada, and she enjoyed playing into that.

"As much neighbors as Canada is to the US," I agreed, laughing.

"My favorite Canadian cheeses, of course, are your cheesy jokes and puns." She leaned in and kissed me.

"Thanks. But listen, I can't remember any of the cheeses you just mentioned, except maybe for the Easy Cheese."

"I'll handle the cheese and the veggies," she said. "You head over to bread and desserts. I know you love your carbs. Man, I have no idea how you can pack away so many carb-heavy things and still maintain that buff figure."

"I have my secrets," I said.

And I immediately felt terrible for even joking about that. I could eat so much not only because my wolf metabolism was hyperactive, but the transformation into wolf form consumed a significant number of calories.

It was one more lie to add to the list. They just kept compiling.

I hadn't worked up the nerve to tell her the truth about my monthly ten-day cycles back in July. And that nerve never came.

Because less than a week later I had to make myself scarce for another ten days. I used the excuse that I had to continue working on my novel deadline.

That lie was easier to work with because I really did need that time. I truly had been behind schedule on the manuscript, and I knew this last extension had already pushed both my agent and publisher beyond what should have been the final straw. I realized the only reason I'd likely gotten away with it was the positive media related to the hype about the upcoming film release based on my first Bronte novel, *Print of the Predator*.

But I was desperately under the gun. Because my nights were spent running around on all fours and howling at the moon, I'd needed to dedicate most of my daytime hours working on finishing the book to get it in for the latest July twentieth deadline.

And yes, admittedly, I didn't really want the writing of the novel to end. Because I had tied working on the book with needing to see Gail for my research on it, despite the fact that we hadn't talked about the book in weeks.

The manuscript for *Tome of Terror* had become, in many ways, a talisman of what allowed Gail and I to remain together. Yes, it had been the initial perfect excuse to keep seeing her. But I'd found it was something I'd clung to. As if afraid that once I handed the manuscript in, what Gail and I had would suddenly end.

But I did turn it in on time. Mack would have likely strung my balls from the door of his office if I'd not come through.

Being caught between that threat from Mack and the threat from Isabeau really put me in a bad spot. I'd managed, so far, to escape both. Despite the ongoing monthly cycle of lies I kept doling out.

Sure, I earned a living making shit up, basically, lying for somewhere between eighty to one hundred thousand words. But lying to Gail, however, was significantly difficult. Particularly when I could tell, with every single story I'd come up with, her trust and faith in me were wavering, teetering on the edge of collapse.

My lie for August had been a need to be out of town to do some pre-movie release interviews in Los Angeles. It had been partially true. There were a number of interviews with Hollywood types, that had all been done via New York to LA studio links and virtually. But Gail didn't know that.

She'd actually asked if she could accompany me on that trip I'd made up. I concocted a flimsy excuse that I had asked Mack if the studio or his office could pay for her to join me but they didn't have the funding. And I'd known, with the repair bills related to the bee incident in her store, she could not afford to pay her own way for the trip.

Fortunately, she never called me out on the fact that I could afford to pay for her to accompany me. But she wasn't the type of person to ever play that card. And she likely would have turned down me spending the money to have her join me.

But the tension between us had continued to fester.

September's lie was another out-of-town trip. This time it was to teach at a writing workshop in Lincoln City, Oregon, run by two book industry science fiction and fantasy veterans—the husband-and-wife team of Kristine Kathryn Rusch and Dean Wesley Smith. The truth was, they *had* invited me to join them as one of the professional writers at a similar workshop, but that was for the following year.

And so, yeah, I felt bad.

"Hey Andrews, are you okay?" Gail asked.

I realized I'd been zoning out again. "Yeah. Yeah. I was just trying to remember the name of those Italian sweet cookies you'd mentioned that go with that...what did you call it? That bruno cheese?"

"Brunost!" She laughed and then shook her head.

"Yeah, that. What were those cookies called? It sounded like pizza."

"Pizzelle."

"Got it." I snapped my fingers. "Thanks! I've got my marching orders."

I did an exaggerated dramatic turn and was about to mimic marching down the aisle toward the bread and dessert area when I bumped into a woman so hard I almost knocked her over.

I had been so distracted—and admittedly confused over the names of the cheeses and other items Gail had rattled off—that I hadn't even recognized the familiar scent of who that woman was.

"Oh, I'm sorry." I turned my head to see who I had bumped into. Her scent and familiar face struck me at the same time.

It was the cold sky blue of her steel eyes fixed on me like a splash of cold water on my face.

"Rachel!" I said, shocked to see her.

Rachel Jean.

Given how similar she looked to Jennifer Aniston, who played Rachel Green on the TV sitcom *Friends*, and the fact she still wore the "Rachel" hairstyle—the one her more famous doppelganger had sported on the first season of that popular program—I'd never forgotten her name.

She never did admit to having changed her name to match the fictional television character's name, but I'd always suspected that. Rachel Jean and Rachel Green were just too much of a coincidence for someone who was the spitting image of Aniston.

Rachel was an actress who took plenty of gigs leveraging her similar look to the celebrity. We had only dated for a few weeks, back in 2004.

I'd fallen for her rather quickly, as I am wont to do; the fact she looked like a television star didn't hurt. And she was a truly lovely person. Perhaps she'd been a bit too much of a go-getter, always dreaming of making it big on Broadway and moving on from the string of commercials she'd been cast for. And she both leveraged and hated the fact her best work came not from her own talent but from the way she looked.

When we'd been dating, we had regularly been interrupted by people thinking she was Jennifer Aniston. She had learned to stop denying it—nobody ever believed her; they always thought she was just rude—so she went with it. She would sign an autograph (in her own signature, not try to fake Jennifer's) and pose for a photograph, completely making the starstruck fan's day but then allowing her to get on with what she'd been doing.

That conflict was something she truly hated. And I could understand it because I'd been fresh into accepting my fate of lycanthropy and what it meant for my life, and hating it. She might have been born looking like Aniston while I'd been bitten to turn into what I became. But we shared that mutual conflict.

Which made her more attractive to me.

Rachel had been the first relationship I attempted since turning into a werewolf. And despite my attraction to her, I never made a move on her.

We'd been seeing one another for three weeks, and, despite being infatuated and in awe of her, I didn't even attempt to hold her hand.

She'd been the one to initiate our first kiss. And what a kiss it was.

It had progressed, rather quickly, to some heavy petting. We were in her apartment and had just enjoyed a late lunch/early dinner she had prepared. It was just hours before sunset on the day before I knew I would morph into a wolf. Because I had occasionally turned early, I was worried about either that happening or the intensity of my passion at the moment making me lose control.

As much as I desired this beautiful woman, I'd been afraid of being there after dark and turning into a wolf.

So, I'd put a stop to it—rather awkwardly, I might add—by telling her I was embarrassed because of my hemorrhoids. And could we wait until they cleared up, which would just take a few days, and just stick to kissing.

Rachel had, of course, been confused, hurt, and a little disgusted that I would even talk about such a thing. But what choice did I really have?

After that idiotic move had killed the mood, I hastily made an excuse to leave her apartment and said I'd call her in about a week, once the swelling had cleared and it would be safe for us to partake in sexual activities.

I did call. And I texted. Repeatedly. But she never responded or called me back. And I'd never seen her again.

Until today.

"Y-you're looking really good, Rachel?" I said. "How h-have you b-been?" I mentally kicked myself for stammering like Bob Newhart.

Her cool blue eyes looked right through me. "Excellent. I've got an amazing gig in Hollywood now. Things have never been better."

"That's fantastic," I said. "So glad to hear you stuck with it."

Gail cleared her throat beside me.

"Oh," I said. "Rachel. This is Gail...my—"

Sticking her hand out and speaking before I could complete that sentence, Gail put on a huge grin and said, "Pleased to meet you, Rachel."

After shaking Gail's hand, Rachel eyed her up and down, giving her a very thorough look-over. I could sense she was disgusted at just how gorgeous Gail was.

"You also seem to have done well for yourself," Rachel said, keeping her eyes on Gail. "But you've also done well for yourself in your career too, so I've seen. Sticking with writing really worked out in the long run. Congratulations on the movie deals."

"Thank you," I said.

Rachel then turned her head back to Gail for another sharp glare before turning back to me. "Did your hemorrhoids ever clear up?"

Of course she had to bring that up. Even she knew it was a ridiculous excuse. "Uh, y-yeah. Yeah, they, uh, did."

"It's water under the bridge now, but all you had to do was be straight with me. If you didn't want to be with me, you could have just told me you were gay or practicing to be a monk, or whatever it was that meant you weren't into me. You didn't have to lie like that."

"I-I'm sor—"

"Yeah, I know. You're sorry. You said that a lot. But you still did it. For such a big guy, you've got absolutely no balls."

I stood looking at her with my lips pressed together, unsure what to say. Gail was giving off a scent suggesting she was about to go into fighting mode, jumping to my defense. I raised my left arm up in front of her to subtly tell her it was okay.

And I also knew I deserved this too.

Rachel fixed her eyes back on Gail. "Has he lied to you yet, sweetheart?"

"No," Gail said firmly, coming to my defense. But I could smell that she was lying. She had her doubts. "Never. And it's going really well."

"Is it? Well, good for you. Or at least he still has you fooled. Don't worry, he'll fuck it up soon."

Rachel turned and stormed out of the deli, each distinct click of her heels on the sidewalk outside an additional small stab to this facade, these lies I was telling myself.

I *would* fuck it up soon, wouldn't I?

Wednesday, October 12, 2011

Chapter Sixteen

GAIL

The sounds of my feet on the sidewalk faded away as I cut over the Seventy-Ninth Street transverse. When I did this run with Ben, we liked to circle the north side of the Great Lawn, but today I was trying to stay as far as possible from any thoughts of him, so I veered right. It was a slightly longer route, but in my heart I knew I would still beat him easily if he was here. Nothing made me faster than being annoyed.

After all this time of texting, calling, and pleading, I'd finally gotten my brother to agree to a dinner out with Michael and me, and then Michael canceled.

Michael. Fucking. Canceled.

My heart pounded hard in my ears, and I jacked up my speed again until the screaming in my lungs almost drowned out the sound of my brain going haywire.

Michael. Fucking. *Canceled!*

Now I would have to call my brother and explain that the dinner I had practically begged him on my knees to come to was not going to happen because the boyfriend he hated had bailed out.

Again.

The palatial facade of the Met loomed ahead of me, and I pounded harder until I thought my legs had caught on fire, and then I ran even faster for the last block.

Must outrun the thoughts.

I made it to Eighty-Fifth, completing my loop, and bent over double with my hands on my waist, gasping for breath. Those people who say they hate running can't possibly understand how well it obliterates emotion. If I had anything left in me, I'd go another ten, just to continue avoiding all these hideous feelings.

When I could finally stand upright, I sauntered back down the block to cool off and catch my breath. Crowds of tourists had taken up their spots on the steps of the Met's entrance, and I was certain I had run so fast that they only saw the blur of my red shorts as I bounded past them. They had probably felt a pop in their ears, a breeze on their cheeks. Maybe they picked up on the panic I was sweating out of every pore in my body, still honey-scented because every moment I wasn't with Michael was spent in our shop. The museum guards would notice the scorch marks on the pavement that weren't there only minutes before. They would all think they'd seen Superwoman.

It's a bird, it's a plane—it's Gullible Gail! Faster than a speeding lie! More powerful than a sexual obsession! Able to leap to wild conclusions in a single bound!

Oh, except my so-called boyfriend didn't like Superman. Only regular guys who visit their family in Canada out of the blue.

After all these months of Michael being concerned about my relationship with my brother—worrying that he was coming between siblings, fretting that I wasn't taking my brother seriously enough—after all that, Michael was visiting his family. He needed to go north the minute he had a chance to help me fix things.

My brother still hadn't explained his bizarre comment from way back in July. I didn't know if the grave danger he'd mentioned meant I'd spend more time with my vibrator than a woman with a steady boyfriend ought to. But if so, he was right.

What could possibly be happening in Canada that Michael couldn't do in New York City? Nothing happens anywhere in the world that doesn't happen in Manhattan; certainly nothing that has to happen tonight. We have entire restaurants dedicated to poutine, for fuck's sake, but suddenly Michael Andrews is homesick? On the very night he was supposed to start a relationship with the one family member I want him to like?

It made no sense at all.

The problem was, Michael never seemed to have anything to do until suddenly he did. He always had these emergencies, and he disappeared for days with no logical explanation. He was "going to a writer's conference" or "doing a media blitz" or something else that sounded totally legit, but he never bothered telling me until the last minute, and then he was impossible to reach while he was gone. I was starting to think I was losing my mind.

Not to mention our sex life was like a roller coaster. Usually, the man was like a hurricane in the bedroom. But when he returned from one of his trips, he was less of a storm and more of a stuffed animal. He only wanted to make out on the couch or cuddle and watch a movie. Which was lovely, of course—I would happily make out with him all day. Once I noticed that specific change in him that coordinated with his trips, I couldn't get it out of my head. Maybe he had a secret family? He was getting super horny thinking about his wife, and then by the time he got back to me, his side chick, he'd used up all that energy? I couldn't think of any other reasons.

I had paced back and forth in front of the museum three times and still hadn't caught my breath. A woman with dark eyes watched me pace, and I had a sudden urge to ask her for help. I tried to imagine how I would explain my situation.

My current boyfriend—wait, is he even my boyfriend? I don't know. We've not used that word yet. My lover? Looov-uuuuh. Gross. My sex partner. Let's just go with that. My sex partner, who I happen to like for way more than sex, is great when he's around, but "being around" seems to be really hard for him.

That's what she said, the woman would reply. At least, it was how I would want her to reply.

Even if we don't work out as a couple, I continued the imaginary conversation, *his publisher is paying me a boatload of money to keep him writing. Frankly, that cash flow is the only reason my business is staying afloat these days. I have to stay on his good side, at least until his next book is finished. Don't I?*

Talking to a stranger in my head was useless. It was time to have a heart-to-heart with Michael. Time to ask him for the truth. This did not have to be so difficult.

Wouldn't everyone be proud of me for addressing things head-on?

I pulled my phone out of the pocket in my leggings and called him. Michael's outgoing message wasn't anything particularly special, but the sound of his voice asking me to leave a message brought tears to my eyes. Why couldn't he be here with me? Why did I feel so lonely for him?

"Hey, it's me," I said, breathing deeply to steady myself. "You really hurt me when you canceled tonight. You hurt my brother. I don't want to think you are up to no good, but I can't stop myself. I want to talk. I care about you a lot, but I've been down this path before—lies, resentment. You know all about all of it. Sometimes it feels like I know nothing about you. But I want to, Andrews. We have a really good thing here. Whatever you're doing, I can handle it if you just tell me the truth. Please, can we talk? Can you just call me? I don't care what time. Just call me. I want to fix this. I want *you*."

I was getting into the "babbling incoherently" stage of the call, so I hung up and put my phone away.

That was all I could do. He would either call, or he wouldn't. I didn't have any control over his response, but at least I'd have a response. With any luck, he'd call me and say, "I'm terrible at keeping a calendar. Let's go over it together so this doesn't happen again."

Worst-case scenario, he'd gaslight me into thinking I was losing my mind or was a possessive bitch.

Well, I supposed the absolute worst-case scenario was that he did have a secret family somewhere else. But somehow I knew in my heart that couldn't be true. Something was going on, but I couldn't see him deceiving me to that extent. Michael Andrews might be a lot of things, but it would shock me to my core if he turned out to be a cheater. Not because I was so special, but because I honestly didn't think he could bear the rudeness of it. It was totally against his nature.

Unless maybe I didn't understand his nature at all?

I turned down his street to catch the subway and was just starting to relax a bit. The run had been a good idea. Every time I got in my head, I could work it all out if I just moved my body. This was a problem with a simple solution. For once in my life, I was in a healthy—if somewhat confusing—relationship with a mature man. I could talk to him. We'd figure this out, and I'd get the God of Thunder back in my bed in no time. After all the fury of the day, my shoulders relaxed.

And then I saw him.

Michael, in front of his building, embracing a woman with a short pixie haircut.

Not just embracing her. They were practically tearing each other's clothes off. It looked almost violent.

In an instant, a dozen puzzle pieces clicked into place.

The woman had been in my store more than once. She had creeped me out when she asked where I was going with Michael. She'd been the one who stomped on our blanket at the park. I remembered him getting freaked out that night when he saw someone, and then everything went wrong when we went to bed.

I gaped for what felt like hours but was only seconds. The woman was clawing at him like an animal, and Michael wasn't even moving.

I wanted to scream. I wanted to beat my hands to a bloody pulp against his building. I wanted to run over him with a car.

I wanted to rip him apart with my teeth.

Instead, I turned and ran, faster than I've ever run before.

He's a fucking monster.

Chapter Seventeen

MICHAEL
11:32 a.m.

"Andrews. Ignore that last message. Don't! Call! Ever! You! Fucking! Monster!"

I lowered the phone from my ear to my lap and looked sheepishly at Anne on my left, behind the wheel of her car. From the sharp heartbeat jump, I could tell she'd heard those last half dozen words Gail had screamed into the phone while leaving that previous message.

How couldn't she have heard that? My phone, held up to my left ear, was less than a foot away from Anne's ear. I'm surprised, given the sharp increase in the volume of that message from the previous one I had just listened to, that I wouldn't have heard that clear across the city when Gail was leaving it.

But I was pretty sure I knew what it was about.

She must have seen me earlier this morning in front of the Algonquin Hotel. With Beatrice.

That made sense. Because I'd thought I had detected Gail's scent a little later when Beatrice and I were getting into Anne's car.

It had been a bizarre whirlwind of a morning, to be sure.

I was walking back home from my obligatory overnight tour of duty as a wolf when I spotted Beatrice on the street outside the Algonquin Hotel.

She was fuming, completely angry, and her heart was beating a mile a minute.

To be honest, I wasn't all that happy myself. This had been the seventh time I had either spotted or smelled her nearby in a public place after that decidedly uncomfortable lunch meeting back in May at Antonio's Urban Kitchen.

While being occasionally recognized in public was something I had started to experience, I had no idea how to deal with someone who seemed to be more of a stalker.

The last time I actually saw Beatrice was at that July Fourth picnic. And that had thrown me for a bit of a loop, likely because things with Gail and her brother Ben had already been tense. But I had picked up Beatrice's scent numerous other times over the past several months. Mostly in public places.

It wasn't like she had done anything like break into my apartment and boil my rabbit. And though it was a city of eight million people and bumping into the same random person a handful of times wasn't likely, it also wasn't illegal.

But here she was, outside my building.

"There you are!" she yelled.

"Beatrice? What are you doing here?"

"Don't you 'What are you doing here?' to me! Where the hell were you last night, Mikey?"

Mikey? Where the heck had that come from?

Her heartbeat was racing even more as her fury escalated.

"You were with *her* again, weren't you? That floozy from the occult shop."

"Stay the hell away from Gail!" I yelled.

"It's true, then! I knew it! I've seen you out with her, but I kept telling myself it was because you were researching your new book. That you needed to be apart from me to work on the book. And that all the time you'd been spending with her was because you were stuck and needed to know more about the occult. I let it go. I gave you the space you needed. But you're sleeping with her, aren't you?"

I picked up the scent of a stranger a few meters behind me homing in on the domestic scene taking place.

"How *could* you? How fucking *could* you? After all that we have together! After the way I have dedicated my life to you! And patiently waited for you while you were finishing off this latest book?!"

Glancing to my right, I spotted a pair of young women across the street who were also paying attention to the scene. One of them was holding up their cell phone as if taking a picture or filming us.

"I love you, Michael. And I sacrificed being with you this whole past summer and now into the fall because I know the world needs your books. And I know that you love me so much that you can't possibly focus on your writing when I'm around. So I made that sacrifice. For you. For the entire world. And *now* look what you've done!"

Oh, man. This wasn't good. When she'd deceived Anne into that research dinner meeting, I knew she was a little obsessed with me. But she was living in a fantastical reality, some bizarre imaginary world where we were lovers.

"Beatrice, listen. I—"

She threw herself at me.

Normally, I'd be able to tell if someone was about to attack because of the telltale quick shift and increase in their heartbeat, and the emotive scent that often came as adrenaline prepared them for a sudden strike. But I had no foresight of this. Beatrice's heartbeat was already racing and the scent she was exuding was like a blinding flash of emotion to my nostril; there was no predicting what she would do or say next.

So she launched herself at me.

It was an odd combination of an embrace and an assault. She slapped me hard in the side of the head with her right hand while her left hand came around my back to pull herself close to me.

She then kissed me roughly on the lips, her tongue aggressively pushing against my clenched teeth, while both of her hands frantically danced along my back and buttocks, performing an odd fusion of erotic caressing and trying to tear my clothes from my body.

She pulled away and looked up at me. "Prove you love me," she said. "Prove you need me. Prove you want me. Take me right here. Right now. Fuck me on the street for everyone to see!"

She started to pull and tear at the front of her blouse with her right hand, and I reached out a hand over hers and stopped her.

"No. Don't do that. Please."

With her left hand, she pounded on my chest, then she pushed herself against me, pressing her lips to mine for a kiss. But this time, instead of kissing me, she bit into my bottom lip, securing a chunk of flesh between her incisors.

She pulled away, her teeth and lips red with my blood.

"Please, Beatrice, stop!"

I reached around Beatrice and pulled her close to me. I knew if I could hold her, keep her arms and face tight to me, she wouldn't be able to harm herself or me.

"Mr. Andrews, do you need me to call the police?" The male voice came from Paul, the doorman at the hotel.

"No, Paul. It's okay," I said.

Beatrice didn't need to be put in jail. But she did need help. I was torn about how to resolve this situation. What could I do? Who could I call?

"Oh, Michael. Oh, Mikey," Beatrice said, practically purring. "You're always about passion, aren't you? When you hold me in your arms, all is right with the world. I'm so glad I agreed to take that money from your assistant, Anne."

Anne.

That was it. Anne. My agent Mack's assistant. She'd know what to do. She always knew what to do. I could always count on her.

"Paul," I said. "Can you please do me a huge favor? Can you go up to my room and grab my phone? It's on the charger on the nightstand beside my bed."

"Sure thing, Mr. Andrews."

"It was destiny for me to be in your arms, Michael. This is where I was meant to be."

Beatrice kept alternating between platitudes of love and sobbing against my chest. And though her heart was still beating quickly, she wasn't acting violent and was relatively calm.

I kept my one arm locked around her, stroking the back of her head as gently as I could with the other, whispering comforting noncommittal words while waiting for Paul to return. "It's okay. It's all right. It's going to be okay. You're okay. It's all good, Beatrice. Everything's fine."

At one point, I thought I could smell Gail's scent. It was faint, as if she had been in the vicinity recently, and I felt a flash of panic. I had told her I'd be out of town visiting family in Canada. And here I was, plainly visible on the street.

But I couldn't stop holding and comforting Beatrice and keeping her in this calm state until I could get help. That was just too risky.

After Paul brought my phone down, I used my left hand to call Anne and told her to meet me here, that it was urgent, and I'd explain when she arrived. I did all that while still holding and comforting Beatrice with my right hand and arm.

Fortunately, Anne lived just a few blocks away. It took less than ten minutes for her to arrive.

As expected, Anne was so comforting and knew exactly what to do, exactly what to say, to connect with Beatrice and keep her calm.

We then managed to get Beatrice into Anne's car and drove her to New York-Presbyterian Hospital, where we stayed for several hours until someone could see her and get her checked in.

Fortunately, Anne had a contact there. She wasn't only the most motherly and compassionate person I'd ever met, but she was also an incredible problem solver. Despite her being so much younger than me, I looked up to her and relied on her advice. And, like this morning, her knowing the right thing to do.

Which is what I needed as we were in her car, and I'd just listened to that angry message from Gail.

"Sorry," Anne said. "I couldn't help but overhear the last part of that voicemail. It was quite angry. And the voicemail she left me this morning—she sounded agitated and upset. What's going on? I thought things were progressing so well between you two."

"They were. I thought they were. She's an incredible woman. Amazing. She's funny, smart, and engaging. I've never known anyone like Gail."

"You really like her, don't you?"

"Yes. I really do. She's special."

"And she likes you?"

"Yeah."

"So what happened, then?"

"There's something about me, something I've never told anyone. Nobody. Not a single person. Not even you, Anne, and I trust you more than I've ever trusted anyone.

"But I want to tell Gail about it. And I've had the chance a few times over the past few months. Only I've kept it from her. I keep chickening out."

I shook my head, looking down at my feet as the car waited at a red light at East Seventy-First Street and Fifth Avenue. Anne's reaction to what I was saying was nothing but pure concern. She wasn't the slightest bit jealous or focused on the fact I had a secret. She was worried about me and my well-being. It hadn't been the first time I'd marveled at her empathy.

"And I've had to lie to her. Multiple times. And one thing about Gail is that she's really perceptive. Really bright. Nothing gets past her. And she has an intuition like nothing I've ever seen in a—" I caught myself before saying the words *a normal person*. "In a *woman* before. This morning, I think she saw me in front of the hotel holding Beatrice, the way I was when you arrived. Trying to keep her calm. I know how that looks."

"That's easy enough to explain."

"It would be. Except one of the lies I told Gail was that I was out of town. She thought I was back home, in Ontario, visiting with my family. That's what I told her. That's where she thought I was."

"Ah," Anne said, "that explains the fury in her voice. She thought you were cheating on her."

"Exactly. She's been cheated on before. Multiple times."

"That's not what your secret is, is it? Some sort of...insatiable sex addiction of some kind?" Anne gave off a thick layer of embarrassment at mentioning that.

"No. Never. I could never do that to Gail. That's not the secret."

"Is it something that prevents you from being intimate with a woman? I don't mean to pry, and I don't need you to tell me. I'm just trying to help you."

"No, it's okay. I get it. I know that, Anne. But no, it's not that. Well, yes, I mean, partially. And perhaps at first. But Gail and I have been intimate."

"Is it maybe..." Anne paused again, extreme discomfort radiating off her as she chewed on ways to express what she was trying to ask. "Performance issues? The mind and heart are into it, but the flesh isn't willing?"

I turned to look at her and saw that her face had turned the most spectacular shade of red.

"No. No! It's not that." I laughed. "It's definitely not that."

"Are you sure? It happens to men sometimes. It can happen to anyone. I can easily get you a prescription to help."

God bless this woman. As uncomfortable as it was, all she ever wanted was to help. Regardless of her own discomfort or the awkwardness involved.

"Getting an erection is not a problem for me," I said. *Lately, I seem to have the opposite problem.*

Anne laughed. "Sorry, I didn't mean to suggest it. But I'm impressed with you. With what you said just now."

"What do you mean?"

"You've never been one for confrontation, Michael. That's one of the most endearing things about you. And it's why you need someone like Mack in your corner, pushing and fighting for you. But you just overcame that habit of avoiding confrontation, avoiding the thing that might make the other person uncomfortable. You did it when you spoke to me about your erection."

"You and I have known one another for years, Anne. You're safe. One of the few people I can talk to. You're like my mother, for God's sake."

"Have you ever spoken about erections with your mother?"

We both laughed again.

"No. Never. But that's different."

"I'm only saying this because you just proved that you can. You can push past that default desire to avoid confrontation at any cost. You'll be able to talk to Gail about whatever it is."

I sighed and turned away to look out the window as we passed the Central Park Zoo on our right. "I just wish I had told her about my secret when I had the chance. She's likely one of the few people I know who not only would understand me, but she'd actually believe me when I tell her. Because the secret I've been holding on to is something most people would never understand. And I've had the chance multiple times over the past few months, but I keep not doing it. I keep chickening out."

"You have the chance now, Michael. Like I said, you've never been good at confrontation. But this is sharing. This is making yourself vulnerable to someone you really care for."

"Someone I love," I said.

Tears came to my eyes. I couldn't help it. The emotions were just too high. I covered my face with both hands and sobbed uncontrollably.

I felt Anne pull the car off to the side of the road, and her arms came around me. She held me like that for several minutes while I let out all of the pent-up frustration and anxiety I'd been holding in.

If only I could talk to someone about my secret. It would be so much easier. If only I hadn't screwed things up with Gail and had just talked to her about it.

"Sorry, Anne. I just realized, for the first time, how I feel about Gail. But it's too late now. I've lied for too long. I'll never make this work. And maybe it's for the best."

"It's not too late, Michael. If you love her, and if she likes you and cares for you the way you said, you have two choices here.

"You can maintain your privacy, whatever secret you've kept to yourself, and lose Gail. Because you can't stand lying to her, and she certainly won't tolerate being lied to.

"Or, you take a chance and tell Gail. And you risk what? Her laughing? Her not believing? At least with that second option there's a chance she won't laugh. There's a chance she *will* believe you.

"But it's not fair for you to not give her that chance. You're taking that option away from her."

Anne was right. So right.

I nodded, feeling fresh tears come to my eyes. These tears, however, were tears of resolution, of resolve. Of course I owed it to Gail to tell her the truth and let her dump me on her own terms, instead of on a misunderstanding based on the deceptive games I'd been playing.

"Okay. Thanks, Anne. You're such a caring and insightful person. I don't know what I'd do without you."

"Don't mention it."

She pulled the car back onto the road, and we drove on in silence, leaving Central Park behind us.

I thought back to something Anne had said previously that I hadn't picked up on.

"Anne, when you were talking about the tone of Gail's voice in my voicemail message, you mentioned something about her leaving you an agitated message. What was that all about?"

The discomfort she gave off was palpable. "She, er, called to tell me she didn't want any more money and wanted out."

"The money? What money?"

"Uh." Anne turned her head as if checking the blind spot in the next lane, but I knew she was avoiding looking at me, even from her peripheral vision. "From helping you with research for your book."

"What?" I thought about what Beatrice had mentioned this morning. But she was manic, filled with delusions, and all over the map.

"Did you pay Gail? And Beatrice?"

"Yeah. Mack needed you to turn that manuscript in, and you weren't making any progress. You needed research help. And it was hard to find someone. So we paid them."

"You paid them? I can't believe it."

"Well, we only paid Gail. The thing with Beatrice fell through, so there was no payment needed. But we kept paying Gail."

"How could you humiliate me like that?"

"As uncomfortable as this is, I'm really impressed right now. Look at you overcoming your fear of confrontation."

"That's not funny, Anne. Not funny one bit. What did she want out of?"

"What?"

"Gail. You said she wanted out. Out of what?"

"Well, after you'd met Gail and gotten some research details for your book, you started writing like wildfire. You were burning through the pages. Gail was having an effect on you. So Mack told me to reach out to her and ask her to keep hanging out with you. We saw how good it was for your writing. We offered her more money to hang around, spend more time with you. And, even after you turned in the manuscript, you had already started working on the next one, which you had never done since we've known you. So Mack insisted that we keep paying Gail while she was having that effect on you."

The car was passing the Barnes & Noble where Gail and I had first met up. Seeing that was like an additional slap in the face.

"Do you know how I feel right now? Like a goddamn loser who can't find his own friends. That my companions have been bought for me rather than earned.

"You lied. She lied. She's in it for the money, while I've been in this for love."

Anne stopped at a red light at West Forty-Fifth Street. I reached for the door handle and opened it. I had to get out of the car and blow off the steam I was feeling.

"Everything I feel is based on a lie! Dammit, Anne. I really liked Gail. How *could* you?"

I stepped out of the car and slammed the door, marching away without looking back. I could not fucking believe it.

Chapter Eighteen

GAIL

I could not fucking believe this guy, marching into the shop with a book in his hands and a pissed-off expression on his face.

Not only did Michael Andrews have the gall to show up in my store, but he had the gall to act like he was the injured party.

As long as I live, I will never get over the absolute nerve of men. Even the ones you think are gentle will act like the Terminator when you call them out on their bullshit.

It was foolish of me to be so surprised that he had the arrogance to show up here today. And annoying as hell that my traitorous heart could still pound like that when I was so furious at him.

"Get out now," I said, "or I will call the cops. I'm not fucking around with you, Michael."

The lone customer perusing the shelf of palm stones looked up, and her eyes darted between us in alarm.

"Go ahead and call the cops," he said, and his voice was as close to a sneer as he was capable of. "They can't arrest me for returning your property to you in a public place."

He took out the copy of *History of the Necronomicon* I'd loaned him and tossed it on the counter.

"Fine, Andrews. There are plenty of women in this city who will fall for your tortured writer act. Go make them listen to your shitty music."

"My music may be shitty, but at least it's real, Gail," he said. "I'm not fake."

I saw the customer pull her phone out of her purse and start recording this interaction. If I had any sense, I'd shut up right now and save my business's reputation. "I'm not the liar in this room. You're the fucking liar, Michael. A liar and a cheater. And you're not even very good at it."

"I've never lied about my feelings, Gail."

"What are you talking about?" I picked up the book and flung it at his head. "Get the fuck out of here!"

Michael ducked, and the book hit the wall behind him, where it splayed open and a wad of cash fluttered all over the shop floor.

"What is this?"

"Payment for services," he sneered. "Anne told me you refused her money, but I don't want you to feel like you worked for free."

At that moment, it felt like the wind had been knocked out of my lungs, and I found it hard to reply. "Are you calling me some kind of whore?"

He ran his hands through his hair and closed his eyes for a second. "No, Gail, I don't talk like that. You would know that if you paid attention to me or anyone besides yourself for even two seconds."

I heard the customer gasp but didn't look over at her.

Michael continued. "But now that you mentioned it, I don't know what else you call someone who gets paid for the pleasure of their company."

"I got paid to help you research your fucking book!"

"Yes, and then you continued getting paid to spend time with me."

I groaned. "That's not what happened, and you know it. But go ahead and believe whatever you want about me. I will sleep just fine tonight, knowing that I'm not a cheater."

"Neither am I!" he roared, and it was so loud we were all stunned into silence for a few seconds.

"I saw you, Andrews," I finally said. "Jesus Christ, the two of you were practically tearing each other to shreds on the streets of New York when you were supposed to be visiting your hoser relatives."

Okay, yes, I admit that "hoser" was a dumb insult. I didn't know any other Canadian insults. Michael may have had a point when he said I don't pay attention.

At that moment, the door opened, and his girlfriend stepped into the store.

"Get away from him!" she spat at me.

Unbelievable.

"Bitch, you better walk your ass right out of my store," I snapped at her.

But before I could make a move, Michael had come between us, blocking me from her upraised arms.

She looked from me to Michael a few times, and then her face creased into a vague smile. "Mikey, honey, dinner's almost ready. I made lasagna. Your favorite." Her voice was thin and wheedling, but he seemed unmoved. Probably because he knew she'd exposed another one of his lies—he had told me his favorite meal was a rare steak and herbed French fries.

Her arms went up to hug him, and that was when I saw the hospital bracelet on her right wrist. I frowned and examined her closer—there was a gauze bandage on her inner arm, where an IV might have been. I looked up at Michael, who had his hands up to block her embrace.

"What's the matter, honey?" she asked, and an edge had crept into her voice. "It's her, isn't it? Is she trying to ruin your work again?"

"That's enough, Beatrice," he said, and my blood ran cold. I'd never heard him sound so menacing before. "You will not go near her. Ever."

What the hell was going on with this couple of crazies? I looked over at the customer, still filming us, and I glanced purposefully down at her phone, hoping she'd get my message and call the cops. She nodded once, and I saw her finger go to the screen.

I was just about to tell them both to leave when I saw Beatrice's face change. She went from simpering to savage in less than a second, her hands came up, and she started pounding his beautiful face.

"What the *fuck*, lady?" I was on her before I even registered what I was doing.

I shoved her up against the store's front window. She clawed at my face, screaming the whole time. I ducked my head, and she grabbed a handful of my hair and pulled. I got my knee into her gut to pin her against the window, anchored her shoulders with my left arm, and used my right to smack her face.

"How dare you come at me in my own store, you little psycho?"

"How dare you sleep with my husband, you slut?" she screeched, and then she spit at me. "He doesn't love you. He loves me. He loves ME!" Her face contorted into a grotesque mask and she flailed against my arms.

Michael reached around me and held her hands down, and a crowd was starting to form on the sidewalk outside.

"Beatrice," he said, and his normally calm voice shook. "We're going to get you some help."

"I don't want help, Mikey, my love. I just want you to come home for dinner. Our kids are there. All of our kids. We have so many children, and they love you so much, and I love you so much. My love, just come home to me. Please."

Her words swam in my head, but I couldn't make sense of anything because adrenaline was coursing through my body at warp speed. I glanced back at the customer speaking in a low voice into her phone, and she gave me a thumbs up and pointed out the window. I heard sirens approaching and finally took a good look at Michael. I could never have imagined this expression on his face—a wounded, terrible fear.

Like a cornered animal.

*   *   *

He took the mug I offered, but I didn't sit next to him on the purple velvet couch. Instead, I pulled up the stool that normally rested behind the counter and sat across from him. The city had grown dark in the last hour we'd spent talking to the police, but I was too tired to turn on the shop lights, so we sat in darkness and sipped the mint tea I'd made us.

"I've never wanted to hit a woman before," he said. "Ever. But when she came at you, I—God. Gail, who am I? I don't hit anyone, especially women."

"There's a big difference between wanting to hit and actually hitting. I know you wouldn't have done it. But she was out of her mind, Michael. You had every right to protect yourself."

"It wasn't me I was worried about."

I nodded and touched my bottom lip. One of her punches had landed hard, and I could still taste the blood where my tooth cut through the flesh.

He took a deep breath. "I would never cheat, Gail. If that's the only thing you remember about me, I want it to be that."

I nodded. "I know that. I let my…" I had to stop and think for a second. I had been about to say *I let my crazy side get the best of me*, but that felt unnecessarily cruel after what we'd just witnessed. "My worst side," I finally said. "I let my worst side get the best of me. My insecure side. I panicked when I saw you with her. I was wrong."

His face was shadowed, and I couldn't read his expression, but I saw him nod. "So was I."

"I always assumed you knew about the money, Michael. I thought it was some kind of industry practice when writers do research." I waited through an agonizing pause before he answered.

"But you kept taking it. Even after the research was over."

"Yes," I said. "I needed it." I waved my hand toward the back wall of the shop, freshly painted but still smelling faintly sweet. "You know I needed it back then, and I still need it now." We both glanced over at the front window where I had slammed Beatrice, a deep crack running the length of it, temporarily taped over until I could call a repair person in.

"So none of it was real?"

"You're not serious, are you? *All* of it was real. Michael, that first day I went to meet you, I was going to take the cash and run."

"But you didn't. You kept playing me."

God, I wanted to weep at the heartbroken sound of his voice. He really did believe it.

"I wanted you. Mainly because of," I waved my hand in his general direction, "you know. Your face." The ghost of a half smile crossed his mouth, and it reminded me of the first day in the café when that slow smirk nearly melted me into a puddle. "I thought maybe we could just bang it out and I could get you out of my system. But then I realized that I genuinely *liked* you. They asked me to keep you writing, and I was more than happy for a reason to spend time with you. I couldn't get enough."

"I find it hard to believe anything about what we had."

"Well, join the club." I set my mug down with a loud *thunk* and stood up to flip on the house lights. I was startled by the sight of him—her blows had left angry bruises on his cheeks. His eyes ran over me, and I knew he was examining the scratch marks across my own face. The EMTs had patched me up with butterfly bandages, but they were stinging like crazy, and my head was pounding. I wished Iz and I were the type of people who stashed whiskey in our shop because I seriously needed to add some pain relief to my tea. "Why don't you tell me the real reason you lie to me all the time."

"I never lied to you about Beatrice," he began, but I held up my hand to stop him.

"I get it. You didn't lie about her. I misread that whole situation. But there is a lot of other shit you have to explain. Starting with why you disappear on me all the time. Where do you go?"

"Gail," he began, and he put his mug down and sat forward, resting his elbows on his knees. "There's something you need to understand about me. About my past. I haven't had the nerve to tell you because—well, it's a strange story. Most people wouldn't believe it, but I suspect you are the one person in the world who would. Because of what you do."

He glanced around the shop, and my heart sank. I'd been through this one before, and I couldn't do it again. Too many people think that what I do for a living gives them an excuse to treat me like crap. So if they chalk it up to spiritual warfare, past lives, chakras, demons, or whatever, I'll excuse their behavior.

"No, Michael," I said. "I can't do this right now. My head is killing me." His face fell, and I regretted cutting him off, but all I could think about was sleep. "I will tell you this: my job is just a job. I'm sorry to disappoint you, but I don't believe in ninety percent of this."

His face was incredulous, and he swallowed hard before he replied. "But you're so good at it."

I shrugged. "I didn't say I'm not good at it. I said I don't believe in it. There's a big difference. I was raised by a woman who put coffin nails in my backpack when I had trouble with a bully at school. She's an absolute nutcase, my mom. Half of the reason I studied occultism in college was that I wanted to finally understand her. It didn't work. But I like my job. Most of it's bullshit, but I still like it."

He continued to stare at me, uncomprehending, and his shoulders sagged as if I had destroyed something inside him. My exhaustion was suddenly so acute that I was afraid I might be sick.

"Now that you know I won't believe any spiritual garbage, will that change what you want to say? All I want is the cold, hard truth. Do you still want to tell me?"

"I do," he said. "Maybe even more." He took a few deep breaths. "But now is not the time. I hope it will be soon."

"I don't know, Michael." I rubbed my temples. "I can't think about this right now. You, or Beatrice, or the shop, or anything. I need to sleep."

He stood up and held out his hand. "Let me get you home."

I stood up to face him and shook my head. "No. I want to be alone for a while."

"Do you think someday you could trust me?"

It would have been so easy to take his hand and disappear into him, to let him hold me, and let all of my problems and worries disappear like they always did when I was in his arms.

"I don't know," I said. "Do you think you will ever believe me?"

He didn't answer me, but instead only shrugged, and on his face was the saddest expression I'd ever seen in my life.

Monday, October 31, 2011

Chapter Nineteen

MICHAEL
8:04 a.m.

How could I possibly expect Gail to trust me when I wasn't even sure if I could trust myself? The past two weeks have been about the saddest I'd ever been in my life. How couldn't I be? I had known and experienced what it was like when Gail and I were together. I couldn't *not* know that now.

Hence the emptiness.

There is a line from a Rush song called "Losing It" that perfectly captures the feeling. They sing about the bell tolling for the blind who once could see.

If Gail had been here, I would have mentioned it of course. And she would have rolled her eyes and asked if I always had a song lyric—particularly a song lyric from some odd and quirky Canadian band—for every possible moment, for every possible feeling.

God, how I missed seeing her roll those beautiful eyes.

How I longed to see that wry smile on her face.

I'd taken it hard when I learned that she originally met me because there was an exchange of money. And I still wasn't sure, if I was being completely honest with myself, about the continued exchange of money, and what that meant.

Her attraction to me had been genuine. That's not something that people can hide when I come equipped with the ability to scent their emotions, their heartbeat.

But even with that evidence, I was filled with doubts. Not about Gail. About me.

You can take the awkward and unfortunate-looking young boy with big ears out of the small town, morph him from an ugly duckling into a swan, endow him with supernatural strength and abilities, and shower him with the experience of fame and fortune. But you couldn't take any of those initial self-perceptions out of that boy.

I knew I was a pretty good-looking man. Gail herself mentioned it regularly. But to me, I was still that big-eared, freckle-faced kid with the at-home DIY mixing bowl haircut.

Imposter syndrome was a powerful thing.

I was raised an only child. I didn't have any friends. I was overprotected and coddled by my mother. She would have done anything for me, and often did.

For my eighth birthday party, I'd invited everyone in my class to come to a pool party — we had a decent above-ground pool, and my birthday coincided with the annual spring/summer opening of the pool. Initially, nobody wanted to come. It wasn't until the last minute that a half dozen of the kids changed their previous "regrets" RSVP. It was a ton of fun. I splashed around and played games in the pool and yard with my classmates, enjoying endless cheese puff, potato chip, and cookie snacks followed by hamburgers, hot dogs, and cake. While us kids played, all the parents sat in the adjacent area of the deck, enjoying steak, ribs, baked potatoes, and an endless supply of beer and liquor.

That birthday had been the most fun I'd had as a kid, and the first time I felt accepted as one of them with a handful of my classmates.

I hadn't learned, until years later, that my mom had called several of the kids' parents and invited them to an adult party, promising booze and food. She even provided and prewrapped the gifts they had all supposedly brought. All the parents had to do was show up with their kids to be part of it.

My mother was like that. She always looked out for me, wanted the best for me, and would do practically anything for me. But it still hurt that my mom had to bribe the kids' parents for me to have anyone come to my birthday party.

My dad, who seemed to resent how babied I was, did his best to compensate for my mom's exuberance. He was mostly distant and seemed to engage with me only when it was time to point out unmasculine traits, or how ugly I was.

He used to joke with my mother all the time, in front of me, that he was convinced I was the milkman's baby because I didn't get any of my father's good looks. I didn't realize at the time that he wasn't just mocking me—he was also being cruel and insulting to my mother.

A story he repeated over the years involved me being so ugly that nobody wanted to play with me; that was why I didn't have any friends. He laughed and said that when I was a baby, they needed to tie a pork chop around my neck just to encourage the dog to play with me. He also used to joke that when I was first born, my ears were so big they didn't know what I might do first—walk or fly like Dumbo.

No wonder I found solace and escape in books and comic books. And it's not surprising how much I strongly identified with friendless nerd Peter Parker.

If anything, I wasn't angry at Gail. I was angry at myself. For believing that someone might actually want to spend time with me because of who I was—and not because I was famous or because someone, behaving like my overprotective mother, actually paid them to do it.

That self-doubt was hard to get past.

Despite knowing—without a single doubt, because those underlying emotive scents people give off are the best lie detectors that exist—Gail really did like me.

And, when we were talking it over, she was genuine when she shared her feelings for me.

But she was also being authentic when she said she didn't believe in any of the paranormal things she based her livelihood on. And especially when she said she just wanted to be alone.

So I'd spent the last two weeks running this endless merry-go-round in my head. I wasn't able to sleep or write. And I didn't think it would resolve itself if I just stayed here spinning.

I gave Gail some space. Not calling her, not texting her, not stopping in to see her at her shop had been one of the hardest things I've ever done.

But I knew I couldn't leave it like this.

I had to be strong. I had to face the situation rather than hide or shirk it. I had to confront Gail about it.

No, not confront.

Anne had said it to me in the car that day. *This isn't a confrontation. This is sharing. This is making yourself vulnerable to someone you really care for.*

I would be sharing the truth with Gail in an open and vulnerable way.

She might laugh. But also, Anne reminded me that she might not. *There's a chance she will believe you,* Anne said. *But it's not fair for you to not give her that chance. You're taking that option away from her.*

It wasn't fair for me to take that option away from her. I was no better than my mother when she lied and tried to protect me from reality.

I had to take the chance, find a way to tell her the truth. To let her know how I felt about her, and that I was okay being one hundred percent vulnerable with her.

*   *   *

2:24 p.m.

The surprise radiating off Gail was twofold.

Part of it was that I walked into her store after two weeks of absolutely no contact—not a single word.

The other was what I was wearing and carrying through the front door.

I'd found a werewolf costume consisting of an open red plaid button-down shirt that showed off a padded furry chest and stomach, hairy forearms, and paws. I wore the full head mask but had strategically cut the snout and eye area to show my face. In addition, I had used black and brown makeup on my nose.

I carried a large boom box with a cassette tape in it all cued up to a song I had selected.

I'd also waited out of sight, outside the store, until there was nobody inside. Because what I wanted to tell Gail couldn't be done in front of others.

Fortunately, standing on the street for so long in that costume wasn't a particularly strange sight to behold because it was October Thirty-First.

When I walked in, Gail stood at the front cash desk wearing a witch outfit. She had an oversized hat with a large golden buckle and a brim width that went out past her shoulders. She also wore a long straight-haired blonde wig that contrasted with the dark of the hat and the rest of her costume. Her dress had a corset-style front with a web pattern on it. The thin arms of the dress led out to overly large poufy and dangling sleeve cuffs to match the giant hat.

She was, at once, stunning and gorgeous.

Of course, she could have been wearing sweatpants, a bulky hoodie, and just-slept-in messy hair and I would have said she was the most spectacularly beautiful woman I'd ever seen in my life.

"Andrews?" she said. Her voice and scent were a mix of surprise and delight. "What the—"

I raised a hairy gloved finger in the air, shaking my head. "Just listen."

I placed the boom box on the cash desk and pressed the play button.

The opening drum beat and piano of Warren Zevon's "Werewolves of London" started up. I started hustling and moving to the music, swaying back and forth, spinning around, and jiving to the song.

Gail started laughing. "Andrews, what the hell are you doing?" She shook her head and watched me gyrate around. The smile on her face warmed my heart more than any beautiful sunset or sunrise ever could.

When the first vocals of the song started up, I began lip-syncing along. As Zevon sang about seeing a werewolf walking around with a Chinese menu in his hand, I reached behind me. A laminated menu from the first Chinese food place Gail and I had eaten at was tucked into the back of my pants under my shirt. I pulled it out and waved it in the air before dropping it on the counter.

I could tell immediately that she recognized it.

When the song got to the part about the werewolf ordering Beef Chow Mein, which was the dish I had ordered that night, I pointed to the menu, where I'd circled that. I had also circled the meal Gail had ordered.

I hooked both thumbs to point at myself when Zevon sang the chorus, and when he sang "of London," I loudly sang "of New York."

I also couldn't resist singing the "Awooo" parts out loud. Because, admittedly, I loved this song and was really getting into it.

When the first part of the chorus finished, I danced around the counter, took Gail's right hand in my left, and placed my own right hand on the small of her back. She gracefully slipped into the dance with me, and we moved about the open area at the front of the store. It was amazing to move in sync with her in this fast-paced dance. But we did it as if we'd both practiced it for years. That's just how natural moving around with Gail was.

As the song got to the second chorus, I rolled her off my arm, and she did a beautiful pirouette, her long black dress flowing marvelously.

Then I repeated the gesturing at myself for the "werewolves" bit and singing "of New York."

My plan had been to do this dance and lip-sync to this song, with my blatant hints, then, when the song ended, explain to Gail that this was exactly what I had been keeping from her. Then I would tell her to think about all the times I'd had to "be away" and how it synced up with the cycle of the moon.

But I never got to the end of the song.

Gail's heartbeat, the warmth, the passion, all of it, kept growing and growing. Her resistance and the internal walls she had built seemed to melt and fade as the song went on. And she kept laughing and shaking her head.

I could scent she suspected what this was all about.

Before I could get to one of my favorite parts of the song, where Zevon says that he'd like to meet his tailor, Gail leaped across the space between us, pressed her lips into mine, and kissed me as passionately as that first time we'd kissed in the lobby of the Algonquin Hotel.

Tuesday, November 1, 2011

Chapter Twenty

GAIL

From where we stood gazing into the Central Park Zoo, Michael and I could have easily walked straight down Fifth Avenue, made a quick right on Forty-Fourth, and arrived back at the Algonquin, the hotel where we'd had our first kiss. I couldn't help but think how wonderful reenacting that date would feel.

Part of me wanted to go. The sentimental part of me, that I usually tried to bury down deep, wanted to take his hand and make a beeline for our special place. We could crack jokes in the lobby and get dirty looks from the other patrons when our groping got too intimate. We would pretend we were there for business purposes, and the sex was purely accidental and purely meaningless. That small, sentimental part of me wanted to recreate every one of our early moments, exactly as they had existed before we hurt each other so badly.

But of course, the non-sentimental part of me, the part that ruled most of my days, would change so much. I would have told him about the money right off the bat. I would have explained that I had more issues than *Vogue* when it came to trusting men.

And I would have demanded explanations for each absence. So much of my agony could have been avoided if I'd stopped trying to pretend I was the cool girlfriend and just admitted how it felt when he disappeared.

It was one of those movie-set New York moments, air as crisp as a McIntosh apple and trees showing off their most colorful couture, all held together by the icy clear blue sky. I could sense Michael wanting to make a joke—I'd have been willing to bet that it was along the lines of "this weather is unbe-leaf-able" or how "grate-fall" he was feeling. Though I normally loved his jokes, even the stupid ones, for once I was glad that he was just letting this moment be.

We paused at the zoo entrance and watched a heavily powdered newswoman intone to a camera that the zoo was still investigating who or what was attacking the animals, and if anyone had information, they should report it immediately.

I felt Michael stiffen, but when I looked at him, his face relaxed and he smiled at me. I felt a gnawing inside me, and had the strangest feeling he had more to tell me about himself.

"Andrews, I want to ask you something really crazy," I said. But before I could ask the question, I saw the newscaster notice us. She cocked her head to the side, and I could practically see the gears turning in her head. We moved away before she figured it out and walked silently for a few minutes.

"Nice day," Michael murmured, looking up at the tree, his voice a study of nonchalance.

"Do you think she recognized us?" I asked.

He shrugged. "I think she thought we looked familiar. But she didn't figure it out."

I turned to look at her, and when I saw that she was back in front of the camera and not sending a news crew after us, I slowed my gait. The video of the incident with Beatrice had, naturally, gone viral. In the weeks since it happened, Michael and I had endured a fair amount of curiosity from the rest of the world, including both compliments and condemnation about how Beatrice had been treated, how the mentally ill were treated in America, and whether her stalking or my defending Michael was the more violent action.

It then morphed into debates about the literary merit of Michael's books and the potential presence of Satan inside my store. On one particularly bad day, a group of Christian fundamentalists staged an exorcism outside the shop. Fortunately, they hadn't been able to muster up too many protestors, and it fizzled out before noon. Iz had done most of the damage control with our social media while I'd stayed behind the counter.

Iz had told me she'd even found some erotic fan fiction online, a love triangle between a horror writer with a cannibal kink, an oversexed witch, and a naïve ingenue with a pixie cut, all set in our store. Ultimately, all the publicity had been good for us financially, so I couldn't really complain. Though I could have done without the internet trolls rating our looks and the online polls debating who between me, Iz, and Beatrice Michael should fuck, marry, and kill.

Michael had far more experience with public attention than I did, of course, but it had rattled both of us. Now that we were spending time together again, I was even more cautious of people seeing us together.

"What did you want to ask me back there?" he asked after a few minutes.

"Nothing," I said. "It was nothing."

It was better that I didn't ask right now. I wanted to enjoy this bubble as long as we could, together again, with New York at her finest. My fears and insecurities and absolutely wild conjectures could stay hidden for a bit longer.

And you don't just come right out and ask a man if he's a paranormal being. It's not cool.

We veered left off the Bethesda Terrace, and he handed me his scarf when he saw me shiver. He moved slowly as he wrapped it around my neck, pulled my hair out of the folds, and knotted it in front. After pulling my coat collar up around the scarf, he stroked my hair and took my hand again.

We'd been cautious with each other lately, as if we didn't know how to be together anymore. He took me out to dinner, walked me home, kissed me good night outside my building, and never once asked to come up. We'd spent my days off on walks like this one, rambling through our beautiful city, sometimes having long, meandering talks, and sometimes just holding hands as we wandered.

"I talked to my brother," I said.

"That's great!" he replied, and once again my heart exploded. How he could be this kind toward a man who had not been welcoming to him was beyond me, but Michael still insisted that family came first. "What's new with Ben?"

"They're having a family reunion of some sort in February. At my mother's place."

"You're going?"

I rolled my eyes. "I'm going. I don't want to go. The only thing worse than dealing with my mother is dealing with all of her sisters. I guarantee you blood will be shed."

"I could go with you," he said, and I squeezed his hand.

"Thank you for that. I already asked. Evidently, this is an immediate family only party." I shrugged and frowned at the pavement beneath our feet. "I still don't know what the hell is happening. Something about finally dividing up my grandmother's property or some other drama. Ben says it's important that I am there in person."

"How many sisters does your mom have?" he asked.

I groaned. Just thinking about it was exhausting. "She has four sisters, and between them they have seven daughters."

He stopped and stared at me. "Any husbands?"

"None that stuck."

"So Ben is the only male in your family?"

I nodded. "Kind of explains why he's so coddled, doesn't it?"

We walked slowly now, and he dropped my hand and put his arm around my shoulder. "I'm glad you're going," he finally said. "If only to spend time with your brother."

"Me too," I said, though I wasn't entirely sure I believed it.

We stopped at the entrance to Bow Bridge where, as usual, a man was on one knee, proposing to a woman who was covering her face with her hands. We paused, waited until she tearfully accepted, and continued our way across.

"I love it when I see those," Michael said.

"I know you do," I laughed. "Stick around, there will be another one within minutes. And another one right after that. They line up over at the south end. You have to take a ticket and wait your turn to go to the top of the bridge and propose. If the woman refuses, the next man just moves up the assembly line. Everyone comes off this bridge with a ring. That's a true story."

He frowned and glanced at the bridge entrance before looking back at me and realizing I was joking.

"Not a fan of public displays of affection?" he asked. "Why am I not shocked?"

"Everyone in New York goes to the same four spots to propose. It's just unimaginative. Their proposal pictures are basically stock photos. Those clones are more interested in spectacle than actually being in love."

"I'd bet that most of them are in love."

"That's because you think the best of everyone," I said. "It's the nicest part of you."

He stopped me at the top of the bridge, looked deep into my eyes, and got down on one knee.

"Andrews!" I hissed, "Are you kidding me?" All of the air left my lungs.

Michael bent over and tied his shoe.

It took me a minute to catch my breath, and I tried to smile at the crowd of onlookers ready to applaud the one hundredth proposal of the day. I was sure by their pitying faces that my expression was more of a sick grimace.

Michael stood up, buttoned his coat, and patted the stone bridge with the palms of his hands. "It's getting late," he said, his voice as casual as if he was talking about the weather. "Want to grab some dinner?"

My face was still flushed, and I started laughing at the sudden, horrifying realization that I had been ready to accept whatever he proposed.

"You idiot," I said. And then I flung my arms out to the side and hollered, "Yes, yes, a thousand times yes! I WILL have dinner with you, Michael Andrews!" The onlookers clapped gamely, though their confusion was still evident.

Michael pulled me into him and whispered in my ear. "Suppose someone wanted to propose something more long-term than dinner. Where would the right place be?"

"Where do you think it would be?"

When he looked up at the trees to ponder the question, I reached my hand up and touched the crinkled lines at the corner of his eyes. The cut on his face had healed without a scar, and it occurred to me that I would be happy to look at his face for the rest of my life.

The thought made me dizzy.

"I think you want me to think it's somewhere creepy," he finally said. "Like a morgue, or a dive bar, or your ex-boyfriend's new girlfriend's apartment, or that sex museum on Fifth."

"I wouldn't object to any of those," I said.

"You wouldn't object," he agreed. "But none of those would be right. Whoever proposes to you has to be smarter about it. It would have to be the opposite of a spectacle. He'd have to make sure no one was watching. He'd have to catch you off guard. He'd have to make sure you were totally absorbed in something you love."

It was suddenly hard to speak. "So, where would that be?"

"A handwritten proposal, hidden inside a Jane Birkin vinyl at Generation Records in the Village. Right after you found it, he'd take you over to Murray's for a cheese board and red wine. Then, he'd take you back to his place—wherever that is—and make love to you by candlelight."

My mouth actually dropped open.

"Or something like that," he said. "I haven't really thought about it."

"God*damn*," I said, and my voice was husky. I cleared my throat and tried again. "That might actually work on me."

Michael smiled. "Should we go eat?"

My heart pounded in my chest, but I knew if I didn't say something out loud right that moment, I might not ever say it. For once in my life, I wanted to be the first to say it, no matter the consequence.

"I love you, Michael Andrews." The grin started on the side of his mouth and then broke across his whole face, and I breathed a little easier. "I am wildly, completely in love with you. I know we almost fucked everything up, and I know we have a lot to figure out, but I want to say it anyway. I want you to know."

"Well, well, well," he murmured. "Look at you. Proclaiming your feelings publicly. On a bridge where everyone in the city proposes."

"Don't remind me that I'm a cliché." I groaned and buried my face into his jacket, inhaling his familiar woodsy scent. "It's this fucking bridge! I swear to the pagan gods above, this bridge is enchanted with some kind of love potion."

"No," Michael said. "It's just a stone bridge. I don't even think it's the prettiest bridge in the city. But it's the best one because it's where the woman I've been in love with since I met her for a coffee first told me that she's in love with me."

And then Michael Andrews, the famous writer, leaned down and kissed me, the infamous occult shop owner.

It was a kiss like our first kiss, when he couldn't get enough of me, and every touch set our bodies aflame. It was a kiss that taught me what it felt like to be loved. It was a kiss that made me forget every single person who had ever kissed me before.

It was, without any doubt, the best kiss of my life.

Saturday, July 29, 2017

Epilogue

MICHAEL
11:04 a.m.

It was, without any doubt, the best kiss of my life.

I could still feel it, not just in my lips, but right down to the depths of my soul every time I closed my eyes. Even now. Even after all of this water under the bridge between us.

So much had happened to separate us. But now, after all this time, we had rediscovered the magic we'd found in one another.

I yawned, my body's quest for oxygen reminding me how little sleep I'd gotten last night.

But even the yawn wasn't able to break the stupid grin I knew I had been sporting since late yesterday afternoon when I finally came back out of the hazy comatose state I had been in for a solid two weeks.

It felt strange to be grinning.

But in the past fifteen or so hours, I'd done a hell of a lot of grinning, laughing, and lovemaking as Gail and I had rediscovered the powerful and soul-fulfilling *us* that we'd first discovered all those years ago and then had spent a half dozen years hopelessly denying.

I had certainly gotten more than my fair share of sleep those two weeks prior. Because even when I was awake and sitting up in front of the television, I was more of a mindless zombie, sleeping with my eyes open. At least the laugh tracks and repetitive sitcom storylines were better than the nightmares I'd continued to relive every time sleep pulled me back down into its clutches.

Sleep was supposed to be an escape. A refuge.

But the same seductive darkness of sleep's promise to take the pain away always led to a horrific funhouse maze of mirrors, forcing me to face what I wanted to escape.

To sleep, perchance to dream. Ay, there's the rub.

Fucking Shakespeare. He captured that juxtaposition so brilliantly.

That promise of escape into sleep consistently led to haunted dreams filled with crystal clear memories.

Of every single action I'd taken and not taken in that final battle.

Of hearing Lex admit what she'd always known about my feelings for Gail.

Of watching her purposely release her grip on that steel railing.

Of knowing she had made that sacrifice to ensure Gail and I lived.

Of Lex's last words.

Say you'll remember me.

Of course I will remember her. I could never forget her. She was a remarkable woman. Meeting her had changed my life. And she would always be in my heart.

I did love Lex. But, as much as I had tried to deny it to myself and everyone else, I still also loved Gail. Those feelings, though buried, had never truly gone away. Lex knew that. And yet she never let it stop her from continuing on, from loving me unconditionally. And even from loving Gail.

As confused as I'd been, trying to pretend I wasn't deeply in love with two women at the same time, I was even more befuddled by how the three of us had gotten along so well.

Lex and Gail should have hated one another.

They should have both hated me for my role in a frustrating love triangle.

And yet that hadn't been the focus.

We had all been dedicated to working collaboratively to prevent the PFA from their growing attacks, from the spreading of hatred, white supremacy, and of fear.

I sometimes wonder if, ironic as it appears, the Proud Fighters for America actually brought Gail, Lex, and me closer than we ever could have been without their threat.

While the larger PFA organization was no longer an immediate concern, a few dangerous members with enhanced powers remained at large. As we'd talked last night, Gail had filled me in on updates from Special Agent Reynolds and Detective Wagner about what they knew and were willing to share with us. It was inevitable that Gail and I would need to be prepared to face them again, and be ready to fight against the evil and hatred that led to violence and crime.

But for now, I was okay with facing what had just happened between us.

Figuring out my future with Gail.

As I scrubbed the frying pan used for the omelet I'd made for us earlier this morning, I made a mental list of the food I would pick up to replenish the fridge.

I had, after all, used up the last egg, the last bits of meat, the last drop of milk, and the last vegetables in the house in making that omelet. Which we'd needed to refill the calories of all of the laughing and the lovemaking we'd done since yesterday evening.

As I was making the list of groceries in my head, I added the things I might need as the fixings for a romantic picnic. After breakfast, Gail had left for the first time in two weeks. She'd headed back to her place to check in on her store. And she planned on returning again midafternoon.

So I knew I had plenty of time to head out and pick up the supplies before she returned. Neither of our previous attempts at a picnic had worked out.

But this one would.

Instead of heading over to Central Park, we would have it here in my apartment. I wasn't done with my rediscovery of every curve, every inch of Gail's magnificent body. And I wasn't interested in either of us getting arrested for indecent exposure or lewd public displays of affection in a city park.

We had so much missed time to make up for.

But our life together had begun anew. And there was no way I was going to let that go.

Being with Gail was like being home for the first time in my life. And I cherished that place with every fiber of my being.

Considering what had happened a little over two weeks ago, considering the nightmare this entire city had been facing, it was an odd contrast to be able to feel the gigantic grin my face refused to let go of.

So, when I detected the familiar scent of the two of them outside my door, even before the solid and measured three-beat knock that came, I should have done my best to ignore it.

I should have covered my ears and blurted out the singsong *Blah blah blah, I can't hear you!*

I should have rushed to the bedroom, thrown the sheets over my head, and returned to the nightmares that had consumed me for the previous two weeks.

I should have dropped the frying pan into the hot, soapy water, gone to the window, and launched myself out of it.

I should have done anything except walk over to the door while drying my hands on the dish towel.

Because the emotions I was reading from the two of them clearly let me know this was not a social call. This was a meeting to deliver the type of terrible news I would never want to hear.

When I opened the door, I looked into the faces of two people I hadn't seen in a half dozen years.

Gail's brother Ben, and her ex-best friend, Isabeau.

"Andrews," Ben said, his face deadpan and darker than I remember the first and only time we'd met at that

Fourth of July picnic. The smell coming off him told me his fear and hatred for me was richer and thicker than it had ever been—as if it had been marinating for all these years. "We need to talk."

I couldn't look Isabeau in the eyes, but she gave off a combination of compassion and fear.

"C-c'mon in," I said, stepping aside. "Is this about Gail? Did something happen? Is she okay?"

They moved inside, and I closed the door.

"No," Isabeau said. "She is not okay. You are not okay. The world is not okay."

"What are you talking about? Where is Gail?"

"You can't see her again."

"The hell I can't," I growled.

"It might already be too late. You two opened up something I've been trying to prevent since you first came into my sister's life," Ben said. "It's not about you two. It's about something bigger. You just undid years of hard work. Centuries of legacy. There are consequences."

"Consequences," Isabeau said, "that go far beyond just the two of you."

My heart was racing, and I found it difficult to breathe. "I don't understand."

"Sit down, Andrews," Ben said. "You're definitely going to need to be sitting down for this."

Coming Soon

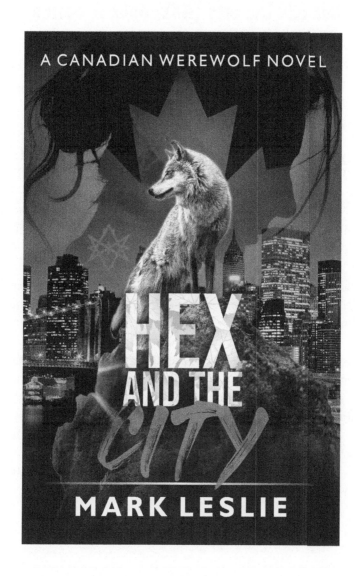

A CANADIAN WEREWOLF NOVEL

HEX
AND THE
CITY

MARK LESLIE

Hex and the City (Next Book in Series)

ONCE YOU KNOW SOMETHING, YOU CAN'T NOT KNOW IT

AND ONCE YOU OPEN THAT PROVERBIAL PANDORA'S BOX, THERE'S NO CLOSING IT

Like Verona, New York is a large metropolitan tourist destination.

But it's also home to star-crossed lovers.

After years of trials and tribulations, Michael Andrews and Gail Sommers have finally found the love that had eluded them for so long.

But that discovery has uncovered an ancient evil curse neither of them could have anticipated. It does more than bring down "a plague on both their houses"—it unleashes something far more sinister that can unravel the fabric of the universe itself.

And it may already be too late to try to stuff those seven deadly sins back inside.

Don't miss this: Sign up for Mark Leslie's newsletter at www.markleslie.ca.

Authors' Notes

If you're a long-time reader of the *Canadian Werewolf* series, then you know I end each of the books with a bit of an author's note where I share some of the behind-the-writing elements.

Several readers had indicated their interest in seeing the details of the back-story of how Michael and Gail first met, which is only mentioned in a few brief flashbacks. I realized, if I wrote it, this story would be an actual romance. Unlike *Fear and Longing in Los Angeles*, which contains many romance elements, this one would be an all-out actual romance novel. I did try, but realized I couldn't do that on my own; so I enlisted the help of a good friend: Julie Strauss.

Since *Lover's Moon* was a co-authored title, either me writing a solo author's note or trying to merge notes from Julie and I together might have short-changed what was great about the collaborative process.

And so, for these authors' notes, we decided to jump into a virtual video chat and discuss a little bit about our experiences writing this novel.

What follows is an edited version of the transcription of that recording.

Mark: Hey, Julie, thank you so much for agreeing to do the author notes in collaboration with me.

Julie Strauss: Thank you for having me, Mark.

Mark Leslie: As we record this, we are in the process of the very final tweaks and edits. The book is just 15 days from release. You and I have never collaborated on a book before.

I need to ask you a question. When I reached out in - I would say quiet desperation, but it wasn't quiet at all. It was chaotic desperation. When I asked if would you consider joining me on this book, what were your first thoughts?

Julie Strauss: I was thinking: "Oh, God, Julie, don't ruin it."

[Both Mark and Julie laugh]

There's actually a funny backstory to this, which comes from my family. I'm not the only one in my family who knows and loves you. My entire family knows and loves you. My son just adores you. He considers you more his friend than my friend.

Mark Leslie: I've actually seen him more in the past few years.

Julie Strauss: Exactly. Everyone in my family has heard me say many times that I hope someday I can write with

Mark. That would be really fun. And then this opportunity came up, and my husband's first reaction was: "Do *not* mess this friendship up."

[Laughter from both]

Julie Strauss: And then I told my son about it, and he said: "Okay, but Mom, don't lose him as a friend."

[More laughter]

Mark Leslie: Well, we had talked about doing a non-fiction book, right? Which we still have on the back burner.

Julie Strauss: I hope this experience hasn't destroyed that option. But I thought it was very funny that my family assumed that I would be the one to screw everything up.

Mark Leslie: Don't they know me?

Julie Strauss: They know your good side. That's it.

Mark Leslie: Yeah. They haven't even seen the other side. But it was my fear too.

Julie Strauss: You and I are such good friends, and we have very, very different work styles. And this was one of the first things we talked about was how are we going to do this so that we don't kill each other?

I told you right off the bat that this friendship is more important to me than any book, ever, in the history of the world. It was just really, really important to me that our friendship always came before the book. And that if we could set up those boundaries to keep our relationship secure, then I knew the book would be really fun. My secondary fear was not writing well enough for your series.

Mark Leslie: Oh, that never crossed my mind. My thought was maybe I would let you down because we have different styles. We have different approaches.

I mean, how did, how did you handle dealing with the chaos of the way I approach writing?

Julie Strauss: I didn't think it was chaos because we were able to keep a pretty tight leash on everything. I think it came down to that first conversation where I had to be totally honest with you and tell you the truth, which is I will not do anything at the last minute. It makes me panic. The anxiety just makes me physically ill. So I had to be clear that I won't work on it the day of the deadline. I won't do last-minute changes. I will tap out if we leave our work to the last minute, and that's when you'll get really angry at me.

It was hard to say, because I've worked with you, I've edited with you before, and you're really, really good at the last minute. You really thrive at that adrenaline of "let's see what happens in this last hour." It's something I admire about you, and I wish I had more of. But I also know my limitations. So, I guess the answer is setting up the fences in advance and telling you, I will be terrible at this particular situation. If you're going to work like that, you need to find another coauthor, and no harm done.

Mark Leslie: And I thought that was fascinating because you sent a schedule. You had a whole month, and you're like, "Okay, here's how we're going to do this the entire month of work." You had it all mapped out. Even my break times, when I was going to the bathroom, when I was going to sleep. All the things.

[Both laugh]

Mark Leslie: No, I'm just kidding. But you had it very organized and very structured, and you sent it to me, probably expecting me to tear it up and say: "Nah, we don't need a plan."

Julie Strauss: [Laughing] I one hundred percent expected you to say: "Let's just go with the flow, Julie. Let's just see what happens."

Mark Leslie: One of the things you didn't realize, or maybe you did realize subconsciously, is I need that structure. I don't create that structure myself, but I desperately need it. So, I needed you to do this book, not just for the structure but also because I've wanted to write this book for about a year and a half, and I've tried, and I could not get properly into Gail's head.

And I've loved your writing so much. I've loved the way you get into your characters' heads. I was thinking: "Hey, I know someone who can pull this off, and I know somebody who writes with a humor that I so admire."

And I thought back to something I purposely did when writing *Fear and Longing in Los Angeles*. The reason I put your character, Tabitha Hamilton, from your book *Prosecco Heart* in *Fear and Longing in Los Angeles* is I love that character so much. I love the scene at the spooky and hilarious brewery you created. I had to do a little Easter egg tip of the hat. It was kind of like this feeling of: "Ooh, I have a bit of Julie's coolness in my book."

Julie Strauss: And *Prosecco Heart* had characters named after you and Liz in it, in that very same scene.

Mark Leslie: Yeah. It had a fictional Mark and Liz, which made this two-author, two-book, cross-over scene a weird sort of multiverse of madness. But no, I honestly could not have done this book without you. *Lover's Moon* never would've happened. I discovered so much more about Gail: her backstory, her brother, and her best friend. I had no idea these people existed, no idea at all. I did have some family stuff that appeared in *Stowe Away*, some historical stuff that I was vague about because I wanted to leave it a little open-ended. But I had no idea. And then I discovered something cool about Michael too, that we kind of talked through. I don't want to give away spoilers, so I'll just drop that right away.

Julie Strauss: I was excited and nervous about writing Gail. I know how you feel about Gail, and I know she's kind of this idealized woman, and I know she's based on your partner, Liz, who we both adore and worship. When I said to you that Gail needs to have flaws, I need to mess her up a little bit, I was really nervous because I thought you would say: "Absolutely not! She is the perfect woman!" I worried that you were going to expect me to write this idealized, flawless character, which is totally uninteresting to me. I like cracked, messy people who screw things up and then try their best to make it right.

What we landed on, ultimately, was that Gail is competitive. She's very stubborn. She thinks she's right all the time. So I gave her these traits and then gave her consequences for her flaws. It would be terrible if you stop liking Gail because of what I wrote. It would be terrible if your readers stopped liking Gail because I've made her a slightly more difficult personality. But I just knew if we didn't add some layers to her, I would get bored, and then the writing would get boring. And, you know, we don't have time for characters who aren't interesting. And luckily for me, you were really, really open to most of the ideas I had…

Mark Leslie: I had my limits.

Julie Strauss: You did have some limits. You stopped me when I went a little too far, but I was incredibly grateful that you were open to me wanting to make her a flawed human.

Mark Leslie: Well, I'll be honest with you. I was very nervous about handing over a character that I had long put up on a pedestal, the same way Michael puts Gail up on a pedestal. Hmm, I wonder where he got that from? [Laughs nervously]

But I think one of the things that was really interesting is I fell way deeper in love with Gail after you created her with flaws, because she is now more concrete. She is three-dimensional. She was somebody that I could see sitting across the coffee shop table from, joking and arguing with at the same time. I could see someone like Michael being madly in love with her and also find her infuriating at times. Like all of those things which happen for real - that's what relationships are. They're nuanced and imperfect. So, I love how you did that for Gail and for the story. I also love that we spent a lot of time talking about the universe this story takes place in because you didn't know much about it – and most of the elements of Michael's world are things that I only had in my head.

For example, in this universe, how many supernatural creatures are there? Yeah, there was another wolf in one of the novels. But are there other creatures too? What is this world like? And we had a lot of discussions that really helped me understand where this series could potentially go.

Julie Strauss: You know, that really impressed me about you and your approach to this work. This is your universe and you've created these books. This is the fifth book, right? You've created an entire world. You've got these characters you love. You've got this idea of where it might all go and how it all began. And it really impressed me that you were so open, and you said, let's just see where this goes. Let's see where the ideas take us.

I've never collaborated before on a writing project. But I would have expected that when you go into someone else's fictional universe that is already well-established and already has fans, things would be strict and limited. I thought that you would say: "Gail is XYZ. And this plot will go 1, 2, 3, and there's no bending." And yet you were the opposite. You were totally willing to say: "What do you think should happen here?"

So that leads to something I've always been really curious about. How can you have such a loose approach to something that you've already created? How do you have so much trust to be able to hand over characters that you love so much?

Mark Leslie: Well, I only have trust in people I believe in. Right? It goes without saying that I'm not going to hand it over to just anyone. It has to be somebody I've watched at work, who I know well, who I understand is going to take the care, but could also be playful and have fun with it, too. That was an important element.

The other thing is that this whole series came from the idea of a guy waking up naked in a park and wondering what he did the night before. And it was meant to be a short story. Everything has slowly evolved and grown in a procrastinator's way. The first book took ten years to write. So it's been with me for a long time, and most of it's never been written down. Our editor has created a guide, and I know you've created some stuff for me, as well as other editors that have helped me. But I don't really have a proper map of the universe. It's all just floating around in my head, which means it's loose.

And that kind of leads me to think about something that we bumped into. We had the backstory on when Gail and Michael first met, knowing that it's a romance, and they end up together as part of this novel. A lot of what we wrote was based on a flashback and texts from the very first book, which was originally conceived of in 2006 when Michael briefly remembers how he and Gail first met and fell in love. We were limited because Michael already kind of outlined their meeting over a couple of pages, saying: "Oh, I met Gail back in whatever, and this is where we, you know, we did this and we went on these dates and we did that."

Facing those limitations, you and I had fun playing with that.

Julie Strauss: Yes. That was fun because then we could do that thing that all couples do: "That's not what I was wearing! That was not what we had to drink!"

Mark Leslie: So diehard readers might say: "Wait a second. Michael said she was wearing *this*. And Michael said they did *that* on the third date." The reality might very well have been: No, that happened two months later. It's the way he remembered things wrong, which I think is important. Because most of the series is told from his point of view. Except for this novel, which has half Gail's point of view, and half Michael's point of view, you've never seen outside of Michael's perspective. So, you're realizing, potentially for the first time, that we're reading Michael's unique interpretation of things. And, like anyone's, his perspective can be flawed.

Julie Strauss: As is hers. I think it would be really fun for your longtime readers to go: "He remembers it this way, but she remembers it that way. The truth must be somewhere in the middle of that." Which opens it up to a lot of things for your readers to think it through as a couple experience.

Mark Leslie: Yeah. And I think one of the things I loved about this process was, well, I'm a "discovery" writer. I kind of know where the end is. In this particular case, as a romance novel, we know that they've got to be together at the end. We had a Google spreadsheet, and went through the ROMANCING THE BEAT structure from the book by Gwen Hayes. You pounded it out quite brilliantly. And yet, within that structure, we had so much fun because of how we wrote it. You would write a chapter and give it to me. Then I would write the next chapter and give it back to you. We had like two days in between where we were each writing. And honestly, opening up my email box in the morning, knowing that I would have the next chapter that you wrote, was just like Christmas. I couldn't wait to see what you did.

Julie Strauss: Oh, for me too! I knew what each chapter was going to get to, but I never knew *how* you would get there. It was so much fun. Exactly like you said, it was like opening a present, like, okay, what do we have to work with today?

Mark Leslie: And yet something we both had to stop ourselves from doing, because we were doing it up until almost three-quarters of the way through, was saying to each other: "All right. Here's the chapter. I don't think it's that good. I hope you don't hate me. I'll rewrite it if you don't like it." And yet pretty much every single time, the other person said: "What the heck are you talking about? This is great!"

Julie Strauss: I know, and we both did it. "Here you go. Oh my God, this is terrible. I'll rewrite it." And then the other person would always go, this is *so* good.

[Both laugh]

Mark Leslie: And we changed some things, right? Like we had the thing that happened in Gail's shop. We talked about it, and we kind of threw it in, and the first one didn't work. So you went back and redid it and, oh my God. Did you ever take it to the next level with the bees. That was just hilarious.

Julie Strauss: That was very fun. My favorite chapter to write came out of a personal conversation we had. Because I was writing the chapter about the first time they slept together. I started wondering what kind of music Michael would have playing. So I think I shot you a text to ask you what music Michael listens to. You and I have a long history of teasing each other, or at least of me teasing you, for loving Rush. I thought, "Oh, for sure, Mark's going to tell me that Michael listens to Rush." **[Laughs]**

And so then we kind of got into this playful conversation about what is a good or bad sex song. And it was a very funny conversation that wrote itself into that chapter.

Mark Leslie: It's funny. You captured the heart of that conversation in such a brilliant way.

Of course, going back to Rush, as I often do, I remember the first time your husband, Joe, and I met. For a moment there, Joe and I just started gabbing about Rush together, and it was like you weren't even there. It was just the two of us nerding out and then later noticing, "Oh hey, Julie. Sorry about that." It was an exciting moment; I was so happy to find a kindred spirit in him.

Julie Strauss: I just sat there and ate my nachos. I was fine.

Mark Leslie: One of the other moments I loved was the scene where they first meet at the coffee shop. In the original novel, Michael talks about walking in and seeing Gail for the first time. And he's just awe struck like the holy grail is in front of him, that kind of thing. He's thinking, oh my God, she is a goddess. And what Gail was actually doing on the phone and texting, all that stuff was just a riot.

Julie Strauss: That was a lot of fun to write. Because again, I like cracked people, and I like thinking that she's having this absolutely chaotic day. And you do never know when you're making an impression on someone. So, it was fun to get into her head. Because I have read the *Canadian Werewolf* books, I know what he was thinking on that day. It was really fun to make the inside of her head a more chaotic space. How boring it would be if she just walked in and went, "Every man in this room is in love with me because I'm perfect." I mean, that's not an interesting book. Whereas if she's thinking, "My life is a disaster right now, my business is falling apart. Wow. This writer I'm meeting is hot. But I cannot go near him because this is a celibate year. Yeah. Keep it together, Gale." Silly her. She had no idea what we were going to do to her.

Mark Leslie: I know. The poor woman. We just walked her right into that trap. Something else that changed about Gail was based on the original artwork I had designed for the book cover. My designer originally had an attractive young blonde woman on the cover, but she never looked like Gail to me. I just went with it cause I was like, ah, okay, that works. But then, when we started to take this book seriously as a team, we needed to come up with who is Gail, really, and what does she look like? And that's when you sent me a picture of Rachel Weisz. You said: "I think this is Gail. Very beautiful but also might stab you if you cross a line."

And I thought, yes, *that's* Gail.

Julie Strauss: That was a really fun moment because I felt like it locked her down for both of us. As soon as we had this image in our head of this is who she is, it got really exciting going forward. All of a sudden, we had this sense of her as a personality. Obviously, neither of us knows who Rachel Weisz is in real life. But that picture, I think, gave us an idea of Gail as a real woman. She's not a Barbie doll. Yeah, she's probably got some flaws, but she's really exciting and sexy and tough. And it was so fun going forward once we had that image of her that we agreed on. That's her, that's the one.

Mark Leslie: Yeah. That was a really amazing moment. And then I think I got all distracted instead of writing, which is what I should have been doing. I went off and looked on image licensing sites to find the right Gail to send to Juan, the designer, to replace on the cover. And after a few back and forths, we found a beautiful woman whose look fit, but with the wrong eye color and hair color. So I licensed the use of the image then sent it to Juan, asking: "Can you put her in a black shirt instead of a white shirt? Can you give her green eyes?"

Julie Strauss: That's one of the first things I do when I start a book is to cast the characters. There's something about getting that picture. Right away, you go, oh, I *know* this person. And then it gets really, really fun to start throwing things out.

You've collaborated a lot with a lot of different authors, but this is your first time collaborating for fiction, right?

Mark Leslie: My first time collaborating on a fiction novel. I've done short stories before, but not a novel.

Julie Strauss: So, you have a lot more experience with that than I do. What are your recommendations for people who want to collaborate to make it a successful venture?

Mark Leslie: It's a great question. I honestly still think that the top priority is having that early discussion and making sure this is someone that you trust. Not just someone that you trust because you know them, they're talented, and you know they can do it. But somebody that you're willing to look like an idiot in front of, and you're not worried that they're going to judge you.

That kind of trust, I think, is important, especially in fiction. With non-fiction, it's a little bit different because you're more removed from the writing. Whereas I find when I write fiction, I'm really deep *in* the writing. When it's non-fiction, I'm a couple steps above it, looking down at it. So I'm not as precious about it. But when it's fiction, you can get precious.

And then, of course, I think the styles have to align. Honestly, when I look at your scenes compared to my scenes—and yes, we all have that imposter syndrome that we still struggle with—but I think your scenes are way funnier and a lot more fun to read than my scenes.

When I read them, I'm like: "Damn, I want to be as good a writer as this one day."

If you can write with someone you admire, what they can do and their talent, you look forward to it. The idea becomes: "I'll become a better writer if I keep working with her." That kind of thing.

Julie Strauss: I had the exact same experience. Every time you told me something I wrote doesn't work, it was easy to change because we had that trust that already existed in our friendship. It never felt negative at all. Every single correction and constructive criticism that you gave me, I had that the feeling that you just made me a better writer, which is such an exciting feeling to have. I loved working with someone who I think is better than me.

Mark Leslie: Yeah. Because you want to surround yourself with people that you have to measure up to. And I think that's a great place to be as a writer because you're thinking: "Okay, I need to work hard at this. I'm not going in half-assed. I need to give this my all because I don't want to let this person down." I think that's a great way to approach it.

Julie Strauss: And I've sort of been noodling on this idea a lot: both of our weaknesses in writing really complimented each other. I tend to underwrite, and I assume that the reader knows everything going on in my head. And I tend to leave out details. And you, occasionally, will underline points repeatedly and over-explain them.

I would say, "Nope, you already said that in the beginning." Or you said to me, "I don't know what you're talking about. You've never mentioned this before." And it was just so cool that we were able to catch the valleys in each other's writing and sort of meet them in the middle. I loved it. It was so invigorating to be able to do that. It was like you could hold a mirror into my own head and I could see how I don't explain things. You were always able to catch it because you do the opposite in your writing. And I just thought that was the best part of collaborating was when our strengths and our weaknesses really meshed.

Mark Leslie: And not just with the things we did in the craft. Our default writing habits kind of helped each other out. They kind of either offset each other, or we blended them, and we found a happy medium. Our processes complemented each other. You need structure and I thrive in anarchy, and we found a unique balance where what we each brought to the table helped the other person. We kind of needed each other for that to make it work. I think it was complimentary craft-wise, but also complimentary process-wise or logistic-wise.

Julie Strauss: Yeah. I think you're exactly right. I think it worked really well.

Mark Leslie: Yeah. This was a really unique experience. I have collaborated before. But I have never done it in such a way. And I know when Joanna Penn and I wrote THE RELAXED AUTHOR, that was a unique experience because we wrote the book the way you and I are speaking now. But I've never written a novel like this, where we basically wrote the whole thing in a month. The two of us, which meant it was only about 30,000 words each. So, it wasn't as demanding as NaNoWriMo (National Novel Writing Month), but we had to also trust and rely on each other through the whole process.

And we were both going through things. And yet, despite that, we still managed to make it work. And I'm still standing here thinking: "Wow, I still can't believe we pulled this off."

Julie Strauss: The fact that we both went through personal catastrophes while writing means that this book will always be a very, very bright light in my life. Every time I look at the book, it makes me smile because I remember being in a hospital waiting room and reading what you sent me and laughing and getting excited. It was something that I got to look forward to during a tough time. This book will always have a very special place in my heart. For the rest of my life, I'm going to remember what a difficult time in my family's life it was, but also that I had this bright light every day. It honestly got me through it.

Mark Leslie: It's kind of interesting. I've always thought that writing has been therapy for me in many ways. I always joke that I write about scary things because I believe there's a monster under my bed, and it's really just therapy, but this book was also therapeutic.

This book also represents a bit of a turning point in the series. I have the first four books where there's like a larger story arc. And then this one is kind of an in-between piece, a bit of a pause before we get into the next bit. Well, we'll see where that goes because who knows what that's going to be? I don't have a plan, but I'll figure it out. I'll burn that bridge while I'm standing on it.

[Both laugh]

Julie Strauss: Mark, if we weren't collaborating, do you think you would have finished the book?

Mark Leslie: No. I never would have finished it if we had not collaborated. No, I never would have finished this book.

Julie Strauss: I wouldn't have either. There was too much going on, and if I was not accountable to you, I would have just said, "Forget it. I'm done."

Mark Leslie: But like you said, it was a bright light. It was something I looked forward to. I treated myself with getting to read what you had written then the day before. And then that would inspire me to want to write something new.

There were a few times where I was very last minute, thinking, well, she's three hours behind me, therefore, the end of my day is a lot sooner than hers, so I can get it to her later. I had to pull that a couple of times. **[Laughs]** But it was a really fascinating process. I mean, I got to the point where I think I reached out and said, so what do you think about working with me on the next book? Do you want to give it another shot? At which point I worried you might say: "Urban Fantasy? Werewolves? Horror. I don't think so. What we just wrote was romance. This was in my wheelhouse."

Julie Strauss: No way. I'm all in. I don't care about genre anymore. This was a blast.

Mark Leslie: See, I still worry you might regret that. But thank you for stepping up and taking a chance because this was a really good time, and I really appreciate having you as a partner for this amazing project.

And speaking of partners, of course, we dedicated the book to our own partners.

Julie Strauss: Our long-suffering partners. God bless them.

[Both laugh]

Mark, I want to thank you because for a writer as esteemed as you are to trust me with your work is just beyond what I could have dreamt of. And I'm really proud of us for keeping our friendship at the forefront at all times. We share the same values in terms of relationships, and it just means the world to me that we kept our friendships so tight and discussed a lot of things that we had never discussed before. There was one point when I sent you that note saying, our friendship's on a new level.

Mark Leslie: Right. We're talking about some strange things here. Yeah. But I think that was really great because we already had a really strong foundation for our friendship, but working on this project solidified it in many ways.

I mean, it was also a fun excuse to talk. Because we got to have a lot of chats along the way, so it was just a good excuse. Like: "Hey, I got to talk to Julie again. That's cool."

Julie Strauss: Yeah. This time we actually had a reason to gab instead of just, you want to meet for a Zoom beer? Now, I guess we're back to that.

[Both laugh]

Mark Leslie: Yeah, I guess so. But, Julie, thank you for joining me on this journey, and thanks for giving Gail a life I never imagined could be possible.

Julie Strauss: Well, thank you for trusting me with her. I adore Gail, and I adore you. And I adore Liz for letting us be nuts like this.

Mark Leslie: Thanks again, Julie.

Julie Strauss: My pleasure, Mark.

About the Authors

Like Michael Andrews, **Mark Leslie** considers himself a beta human. However, unlike his fictional character, Leslie doesn't have an alpha-wolf persona, despite hair growing on his aging body in all the wrong places.

Mark lives in Southern Ontario and can most likely be found behind the keyboard, with his nose stuck in a book, tracking and enjoying craft beer, or sharing musical earworms and dad jokes.

You can learn more about him at **www.markleslie.ca**.

Julie Strauss is a writer, editor, and podcaster who lives, reads, writes, cooks, and gardens in Southern California with her family.

She is known in some circles as "that weird bookish lady who talks to her plants" and in other circles as "that foul-mouthed wine drinker who laughs at inappropriate moments." She loves you as a person but does not care about your cats unless you have taught them how to talk.

You can learn more about her online at www.juliewroteabook.com.

The Canadian Werewolf Series

This Time Around (Short Story)

A Canadian Werewolf in New York

Stowe Away (Novella)

Fear and Longing in Los Angeles

Fright Nights, Big City

Lover's Moon (*with Julie Strauss*)

Hex and the City

Selected Books by the Authors

Mark Leslie

Fiction
Evasion
I, Death
One Hand Screaming

Non-Fiction Paranormal
Haunted Hamilton
Spooky Sudbury
Tomes of Terror
Creepy Capital
Haunted Hospitals
Macabre Montreal

Julie Strauss

The Oro Beach Series
Almost Blue
Ruby Tuesday
Goodbye Yellow Brick Road

The Chefs in Love Collection
Hungry Heart
Moonstone Heart
Prosecco Heart

Made in the USA
Monee, IL
25 February 2023

28666491R00174